Orphans in the Barn
Seven Not-So Deadly Sins

David Xu

Mountain View Press—Ashland, PA
ISBN: 978-0-9999035-0-6
Library of Congress Control Number: 2020907904
Title: *Orphans in the Barn: Seven Not-So Deadly Sins*
Author: David Xu
Digital distribution | 2020
Paperback | 2020

This is a work of fiction. The characters, names, incidents, places, and dialogue are products of the author's imagination, and are not to be construed as real.

Other books by David Xu

Easy Eddie Books One, Two, Three

Redneck Dystopia

Sold on Amazon Books
EBook or Paperback

Dedication

This book is dedicated to all the orphans in the world. They add so much to our cultures and lives. Everyone deserves to love and be loved. The caretakers at the orphanages are the greatest folks for nurturing the children into fine adults. Let us all help them to leave the dark behind and enter the light and be prosperous and happy.

The orphans learn to overcome so much and thrive in order to reach great heights. Christians are strong and will always triumph. There will always be a void, but they move on courageously. We are so lucky to have all of them. God bless the orphans and America!!

Table of Contents

Introduction

This is a fictional tale about seven orphans from Hershey living in coal country in the mountains of Pennsylvania. They have loved and supported each since bonding at an orphanage. They struggle with not knowing about their parents and with the seven deadly sins like the rest of us. Thank goodness the sins are not so deadly anymore because the state and religion were separated in most places long ago.

The Desert Fathers lived, preached, and wrote in the Middle East about 2,000 years ago. Many of them were illiterate, but not Evagrius Ponticus. He was a Christian monk and writer who lived from 345 to 399 AD in Egypt. (1)

His claim to fame was a comprehensive list of eight evil thoughts. These temptations were to be avoided at all cost. The eight patterns of evil thought were gluttony, lust, greed, sadness, despondency, anger, vainglory, and pride.

Evagrius liked to cry. He thought tears represented true repentance for bad thoughts or behavior. He and his pals would sit around and cry for days to open themselves up to God.

Bubba Watson, the golfer, would fit right in with this bunch. He enjoys a good cry after winning tournaments on the PGA tour. Nancy Grace would be at home with Evagrius also.

Later in 590 AD, Pope Gregory I revised the list for the Catholic Church down to seven sins. This list is more famous nowadays as the "Seven Deadly Sins."

The list I will use for this book is as follows: pride, greed, lust, envy, gluttony, wrath, and sloth. If they were good enough for Gregory, they are good enough for me.

I have always been fascinated that the church and state regimes used to put folks in jail or worse for these sins. It gives me a renewed respect for Thomas Jefferson and his demands for separation between church and state in the great United States of America.

We all experience behaviors, habits, and speech that we disagree with from time to time. Most Christians try to follow the teachings in the Bible. Most Muslims try to adhere to the Koran. This book is a fictional account of some kind and Christian folks in the mountains of Pennsylvania having a great life and dealing with good, bad, and odd behavior.

Most of us struggle with some of the seven deadly sins. Thank goodness we are no longer thrown in jail or worse for our mistakes. It is one of the safest times to live for the human being. Violent folks used to roam freely not that many years ago. It is rare to die a violent death anymore.

The church and state used to be one and the same. It could imprison or kill people with impunity. I remember reading about the young guy who was boiled in oil in the public square on direct order of the Pope many years ago. Thank God those days are over!

Dave

Chapter One
Pride- Pat

"In reality, there is perhaps no one of our natural passions so hard to subdue as pride," Benjamin Franklin. (2)

Pride is an emotional state deriving positive affect from the perceived value of a person or thing with which the subject has an intimate connection. (1) Some folks think pride is a bad thing and others think of it as a virtue.

The Roman Empire was the dominant political and military force during the early days of Christianity, with the city of Rome as its foundation. (4) The Emperor did not care if you had two or twenty gods, but he did care if he was not one of them. The pride of Christians about two thousand years ago got them into trouble and jail or worse. The monotheistic Jews and Christians were persecuted if they expressed too much pride in their religions and allegiances.

April 2019
  Ashland, PA

Vivian and Zeb Brown own and run a farm in Ashland, Pennsylvania. They bought twenty acres 22 years ago in 1998 and love the farmer's life. They grow corn and soybean and have a barn full of cows and pigs and horses. They loved the fact that the property has two gigantic barns in great shape with electricity, water, and sewer. The barns are bright red and white.

They love the three acre yard around the house. The grass is beautiful green during the warm months and spectacular white with snow during the cold months. The wide open spaces just really do it for this couple. They saw a baby deer with bright white spots and beautiful brown fur by the barn just last week. She could barely walk or run and the mother was nowhere to be seen.

The forest covers about five acres with trees reaching sixty feet in the sky. They walk on the trails about every day on gentle hills and valleys. It is a great place to clear your head and think positive thoughts.

Deer, ducks, geese, and foxes run through the farm every day. It lifts the soul to watch them dance around. The deer run so fast and jump over bushes and fences with such ease. God made quite a paradise here on Earth. Many people like to watch the ducks and geese at the pond.

The Muscovy ducks love to dig and suck around in the mud to look for worms and insects. They enjoy this activity for hours and become covered in mud. After a while they take a dip in the pond to clean their white feathers and red beaks.

There are about twelve acres of corn and soybean fields that pay the bills. It is rewarding work for the couple after decades in the Army and the IT world. Their food feeds many folks through the grocery stores.

Every few days a loud siren goes off. Zeb called 911 the first time he heard it. It signals to rescue squad members the emergence of an emergency. They should drive to the station when they hear it. Vivian wonders why they do not get beepers instead. Perhaps they have cell phones.

There is an empty hospital one mile from the farm. It shut down a few years ago and used to serve coal miners and others. The former administrator went to jail for stealing funds. It is a very nice brick building and has six stories.

The executives had a good time renovating their office suites and having lunch parties before running the place into the ground. A group from California tried to buy it and start an inpatient drug rehabilitation center, but the deal fell through.

They met in college at Virginia Tech back in 1976. Vivian grew up in China, emigrated to the United States, and earned a master's degree in information technology on a student's visa. She loved America so much that she earned her citizenship in 1978. Zeb earned an MBA with a dual focus of finance and agriculture.

Vivian is a strong woman who expects a lot from herself and others. She is full of tenderness when the moment calls for it. She is extremely self-controlled and very determined to accomplish her goals. She remembers the hard times in China and appreciates the good times in America.

When she left China, it was a man's world. Vivian loves the equal rights culture and legal system in America. Immigrants see that America is about individual freedom and China is about government control, corruption, and power. She thrives on hard work and success in the IT world.

They met at a Bible study on campus that Vivian had enjoyed for years. Zeb realized he had a drinking problem and turned to The Bible for help. They both believe strongly in God, Jesus, The Bible, and helping others. Their faith is strong.

Zeb struggles with too much pride. He is proud of everything he and Vivian have accomplished and have. Sometimes he is punished for this excessive pride from acquaintances or friends thinking it is just too much. He comes across as arrogant sometimes.

They had a son and have enjoyed the married life for many years. Zeb pulled twenty years in the Army and Army Reserve and Vivian has a great job working with Java software.

Their only son is a medical doctor treating poor people in Africa. He is married to a wonderful nurse who helps him.

Zeb loves Vivian's quick wit and biting comments. She is nobody's fool and a man eater in a playful and charming way. She takes no crap from anyone because she does not have to due to tremendous success in the land of the free.

Zeb's younger brother Steve died a long time ago at twenty years old in a car accident. Zeb was devastated and held tight to God, family, and friends. Vivian and Zeb are old school and never talk about it.

Zeb retired from the Army in 1998 and they bought the farm in Ashland. Vivian continues to work with Java software. Many large companies use the software.

Zeb misses his brother Steve so much and being around young people. Vivian had the great idea to build apartments and rent out their huge barn to some young workers. Now they have seven renters in their twenties renting one bedroom apartments upstairs in the barn.

All the renters met each other at the Hershey School for Orphans. They are all orphans and bonded at the school and afterwards at reunions and vacations. They are like brothers and sisters and very loyal to each other. Many stay connected throughout their entire lives. Some play golf together and others go out to eat all the time. The school helps them find jobs, alumni chapters, and apartments forever.

Pat is twenty-eight and is a very successful physician's assistant down in Pottsville. He has dated many young ladies, but still looking for the right one. He is Native American and very proud of his heritage.

Pat is always looking for approval and recognition. He and the other orphans used to talk about this all the time at their orphanage as children. He still struggles with this impulse and tries not to overdo it. He works extremely hard partly for this reason.

He wears American Indian jewelry and attends cultural events down in Washington, DC at the Smithsonian's National Museum of the American Indian. Pat gets upset sometimes from reading or hearing ignorant people stereotype his group as all being drunk or lazy. He barely drinks and works very hard to fight this stereotype.

Pat is very knowledgeable about the mistreatment of the Native Americans back in the 1830s. The government folks took their land, killed many, and made about 60,000 move west of the Mississippi River. This is one rare example of the United States doing something horrible. He gets angry when discussing this history.

Pat gets nervous with small talk sometimes. He blurts out insults about other people's stuff without even realizing it. He means no harm and just engaging in chitchat. Sometimes his pride just gets in the way of great conversations.

The last girlfriend Betty grew tired of Pat's self-idolatry. He loves himself just a little too much and others sense it pretty soon after meeting him. He has beautiful, think black hair, big muscles, and baby smooth skin. The last straw was a conversation they had while walking through the Locust Lake State Park.

"I thank God that we are doing so well. The money is great with my job and that diesel Ford F250 rocks for only $52,000. What a steal!" Pat said.

"Yeah, this park is a beautiful place to walk. Do you want to volunteer at the church to feed the homeless next month?" Betty replied.

"Maybe, but those people should work harder and buy their own food. I hope you can get a better job and make more money too," Pat said.

"You are such a jerk. Many of the poor folks are victims of horrible people and situations. We should always help them," Betty said.

She ruminated about his stinging comments for hours. They walked in silence in the beautiful park and broke up the next day. She is trying to find someone who loves others more.

In Judaism, pride is called the root of all evil. Proverbs in the Bible considers pride a sin. (1) Either way, it can definitely lead to some stinging comments that turn others against you.

Pat is looking long term at his life. He is powering through the relationships with women and saving money for a nice house and retirement. He does not reflect on his weaknesses such as praising himself too much.

His boss loves his self-confidence and the way he can trust Pat to accomplish any task ahead of a deadline and under budget. He is extremely dependable and puts any boss at ease to delegate responsibility at any time.

Pat loves the way his boss calls everyone a 'Pansy Ass' if they complain about anything. Pat never complains and thanks God for the great job and life on the farm with Vivian and Zeb.

Zeb is blaring a Marshall Tucker Band song on the stereo in the barn. "Can't You See?" can be heard all over the farm. He installed many speakers inside and outside both barns and loves rock and roll music. Pat loves rock and roll also. Zeb gives him music from the 1970s all the time.

Pat sees Ginger beside the barn smoking a cigarette and laying out in the sun. It is a sunny April morning here in coal country. The winter has broken and the sun feels so warm on the skin.

"What are you doing today? It is such a pretty day. Thank goodness winter is over," Ginger said.

"Not much, I need to change the oil in the truck. It needs a wash too. Would you like to shoot the crossbow?" Pat replied.

"Sure, I have never tried it, but it looks fun. I shot a pistol a couple years ago with Pete and that was fun," Ginger said.

"Yes, I am an expert with the pistol too. Did I tell about shooting with the Boy Scouts at Fort AP Hill in Virginia a long time ago?" Pat said.

"Yes, you told me many times how you hit the target twenty out of twenty times and won the trophy for your age group," Ginger said.

They set up the target behind the barn. It is two feet by two feet wide and basically a hay bail covered with canvas with a circular target on both sides. It is one foot thick and brightly colored.

"Look through the scope and put that green dot on the center of the target," Pat advised.

"This laser scope is awesome. It is very pretty. Should I put my nose on the back of the scope?" Ginger asked.

"No, keep your nose back a bit. It will kick a little and skin your nose if you are not careful," Pat said.

"Is that why your nose had a scab on it last week? I thought you had a big pimple," Ginger said.

"Yes, I put my nose against the back of the scope and the crossbow came back and cut my nose. I was still very handsome with the damaged nose," Pat said.

"You can talk some trash can't you? How is Betty doing?" Ginger.

"Well, we kind of broke up. We just did not see eye to eye on some things. I have my eye on the girl at the Dutch restaurant now. Have you seen the one with long black hair and nice calves?" Pat inquired.

"I am sorry, but I do not notice the calves of women. You are too picky," Ginger said.

"I know, I know, but I know that I do not want to get married any time soon. I am so glad to be able to afford that sweet truck over there," Pat said.

"I think you may love yourself just a little too much," Ginger said.

"They say you must love yourself before you can love others. Now I like that old cliche," Pat said.

They have fun shooting the crossbow all morning behind the barn. The birds are chirping and a baby deer ran through the corn field. The sun feels so good after the cold winter. The low temperature back in January was minus four degrees.

Ginger and Pat are like siblings or cousins and love each other. She tries to tamp down his ego and pride, but realizes that is who he is. He has figured out life and making money. She admires his long term view and financial strength.

She knows that he will find true love and be fine in the free United States of America. You can be or do anything here if you work hard and look long term. His self love is kind of cute and he is a loving and giving person.

"I am trying to quit smoking, but it is hard. I have been smoking since high school," Ginger said.

"Well, it is hard to quit. I used to smoke some and used chewing gum to quit. Every time I wanted a cigarette I just had a piece of gum," Pat said.

"I did not know you ever smoked. That is great that you quit. Maybe I will try the gum thing," Ginger said.

"I never smoke that much. I only had five or six cigarettes per day, but I remember that it was hard to quit," Pat said.

"Some of my friends gained weight when they quit. I cannot handle that. Pam looked like a tick after she quit smoking. I am not going to look like a tick," Ginger said.

A squirrel runs by them and scales the side of the barn. It runs up the side of the barn like Spider-man. He disappears between the rough wood boards.

"Wow, it looks like he has glue on his feet. He is amazing," Ginger said.

"Yeah, I think I heard him scratching around above my room last night. I bet he has some nuts up there. I will run him off soon," Pat said.

None of the twenty somethings know what happened to their parents. The kids were dropped off at the orphanage like a package from Amazon. This is what they were told.

They all feel an emptiness deep down inside of being unwanted. That is one reason they bonded and keep in touch with other orphans from Hershey. This is their family. These are their siblings and cousins from different DNA. They are so full of love and tenderness.

"Be completely humble and gentle; be patient, bearing with one another in love," Ephesians 4:2.

The leaders and teachers at the Hershey School for Orphans raise the kids in love and with the Bible. The spirit of love and Jesus are all around them for many years. Most of the orphans grow up to be very successful and happy. God works in mysterious ways for sure.

The neighbor's kid rides past in his go kart with "Long Train Runnin'" blasting from the Doobie Brothers. These folks in coal country love rock and roll music.

"Did I tell you about the pervert at the retirement home where I volunteer? That was hilarious," Pat said.

"No, is the pervert old or young? I hope you do not describe an old one because I just love to listen to the old people. They love to talk to younger people too," Ginger said.

"I was in the bathroom at the Christian retirement home in Reading and one of the residents was bragging about watching porn," Pat said.

"This is crazy. How old is he? What did you say?" Ginger asked.

"He looks to be about fifty years old. He is mentally challenged. He asked me what I was going to do with my paycheck. I guess the employees got paid that day. It was a Friday. I told him that I do not want money for helping him and the others," Pat said.

"Wow, it would have been easy to give him a lecture about that filth," Ginger said.

"I did tell him that I do not watch that stuff and it is a bad thing to do. I had to get that out," Pat said.

Pat later saw his team leader for the volunteer job in the maintenance department. He complained that he is working for free to help these poor folks and this guy is watching porn all day.

"Well, he has many mental and physical problems. You are helping all of these people with your volunteerism. I thank God for you," the team leader tells Pat.

"Okay, but I am not volunteering for the pervert any more. I am here to help the other poor people, but I cannot support a pervert. Perhaps you can get that guy a job or at least counseling. Tell him not to share that crap with volunteers," Pat said.

"The shot hits the bird that pokes its head out," Chinese proverb. Take the middle road. Do not try to be a hero unless necessary.

Pat thinks back to his mission trips to Montana while he was in college. Twenty students and a few preachers would drive out west to help the poor American Indians. Many of the people on the reservations abuse alcohol and drugs. Poverty is severe and educational levels are low.

"I remember seeing houses with holes in the roof. Driving down the country roads we would see people in the houses without windows or doors. The folks live like that," Pat said.

"That is so sad. I wonder why they cannot rise up. I guess it is hard to escape from a poor or dysfunctional house and home," Ginger said.

"Yes, those kids have it rough. We gave them school supplies, Bibles, and clothes. Some of the parents do not trust strangers. They look at you like you are a threat," Pat said.

"That is terrible. God help the children. Let them be Christian and strong. Our federal government with our taxes still gives most American Indians free health care. That has been going on a long time," Ginger said.

"The tribal leaders and parents need to stand up and work hard like we do over here. The Indian Health Service (IHS) provides health care to about 2.2 million American Indians in 36 states right now," Pat said.

"You are sweet to help them. The Bible says we should always help the needy. Thank God we are strong enough to help anybody," Ginger said.

"One day we were driving down a county road outside of Billings on a reservation. We were in a rental car. I saw an arch above a dirt driveway and took a picture. The next thing we know this lunatic was chasing us in a dilapidated pickup truck," Pat said.

"Really? I bet you were scared. What did he do? I would call 911," Ginger said.

"He pulled up beside us on the two lane road. We are now driving two by two down a two lane road at sixty miles an hour. We rolled down the window to see what he wanted," Pat said.

"Why are you taking pictures of my house? I do not want anyone taking pictures of my son," the guy in the truck yells.

"I just loved the arch above the driveway. That is all. We are tourists and missionaries," Pat yells to the stranger.

The guy slowed down and turned around and drove back home. Pat and the other missionaries were so relieved that he did not shoot them.

"That is wild. I wonder why he was so concerned about photographing his kid," Ginger said.

"I do not know and I did not want to find out. This guy looked deranged. He was balding and dirty and I think I saw guns in the truck," Pat said.

The arch is made of logs above the start of the driveway and next to the public road. The dirt driveway leads to a single wide mobile home that looks like it is going to fall down. The front door is open and mold is all over the vinyl siding.

Times are hard for this family. Many broken whiskey bottles are piled up in the front yard. The roof is missing many shingles and the ones remaining are worn thin. Empty beer cans surround the fire pit. Junk cars are next to the mobile home.

Silhouettes of the family can be seen though the open windows. The temperature is 100 degrees. Old appliances and lawn mowers are in the yard. Chickens and a couple skinny dogs roam freely.

Pat feels an affinity with his fellow Native Americans. He studied very hard in college to avoid poverty and have a great life. He will always help his people and wonders why they do not work hard and rise up in the great and free United States of America. He wonders why they do not move away from the poverty and dysfunction of the reservation.

He wonders where he was born. Perhaps he was born right there in Montana. Maybe his parents gave him up for adoption because money was tight. Perhaps his mother was single with no home. Was his father an abusive alcoholic?

Pat is so glad that he had a great life at the orphanage with love and God around every day. He graduated from college and has a great job. He knows his life could be brutal like the kids in Montana with drunk or lazy parents.

"Let us say a prayer. Thank you God and Jesus for a wonderful life. Please help those less fortunate and promise to do that forever," Ginger said.

"Amen, God help the kids. They suffer so much with bad parents in poverty. Do you want to know who your parents are?" Pat said.

"I could go either way. I think sometimes that they could be terrible people who you would never want to hang around. How could they give away a baby?" Ginger asked.

"I think I want to meet them. I wonder if they are still alive. Wouldn't it be wild if they live in Montana where we went on the missions trips?" Pat asked.

"Did that guy in the truck look like you? I am just joking. I would hate to see that guy chasing me down the highway," Ginger said.

"It was shocking. I was thinking if this nut tries to block the road, I am not stopping. I thought he may be a violent criminal on drugs. He had the crazy eyes," Pat said.

"I know what you mean. Well it sounds like you handled it well and de-escalated the situation. I bet that was intense for sure," Ginger said.

"Thank God he was not violent. Maybe his son was bullied at school. Or perhaps he is disabled. I never saw the kid when I took the picture. I am so glad that he did not point a gun at us," Pat said.

Back at the barn Zeb and Vivian are talking on the lower porch of their house. The house is two-story with an upper and lower covered porch. They love to sit in the rocking chairs and read or chat.

"Did I tell you about my grandmother at the liquor store? That was a good one," Zeb asked.

"No, was she your father's mother? You said she was a great cook and a very nice Christian lady," Vivian said.

"Yes, she was awesome and helped me so much. She took me to the mall and bought my first suit for a job interview after college. She was a teetotaler and tried to get my father not to drink. We talked about the lessons in the New Testament all the time," Zeb said.

"She sounds wonderful. It is hard to ignore all the nasty people and she was great for that. God is great. We need more God, Jesus, and the Bible in this world," Vivian said.

"Yes, for sure. Well my dad drove past the liquor store in Danville, VA on the way to work and saw a line in front waiting for the store to open. To his shock, he saw his mother in the line with the bums. He had to turn around and see what was going on," Zeb said.

"The government run store was in a bad part of town. She was dressed in an expensive dress, with fine jewelry, and high heels. The bums were very interested to chat with this old lady. She told me that she desperately wanted some vodka to cook with," Zeb said.

"That is funny. I guess she did not consider the danger of the neighborhood or the alcoholics or drug folks. Why does the government own liquor stores in Virginia?" Vivian inquired.

"That is dumb. It is because the politicians are addicted to the tax money. Many operations should be downsized or in the private sector to reduce the size of government and to reduce corruption and taxes for the working people," Zeb said.

"You told me that your grandmother corrected your English in high school. Was she gentle in teaching you? You were lucky to have such a loving and caring grandmother," Vivian said.

"Yes, she was very gentle. I remember when she taught me to never put 'at" at the end of a sentence. It sounds so bad when I hear that now," Zeb said.

"I think it would be a better world now if the young and the old spent more time together. But now the young are online entirely too much and ignore the old and their wisdom," Vivian said.

"That is a shame. I love to talk with old people. You can learn so much from them. And they love to speak with younger folks. I love their long-term perspective," Zeb said.

"What was that joke? The difference between a statesman and a politician is that one plans for the next generation and the other plans for the next election," Vivian said.

A wind gust blows some leaves past the porch where they are sitting. The leaves swirl upwards in a circle. It is a mini cyclone and a wonder. They fall to the grass when the gust weakens. The sun is out and the sky extremely blue.

They gaze at the mountains surrounding their farm. The trees on the farm in foreground are green and bushy. The trees on the mountains are brown, but turning green with the change of weather. Hawks are flying around looking for a snack.

The sound of chainsaws echo through the trees. Perhaps the neighbors are cutting up trees that fell during the winter. It takes about a year on the ground for the trees to dry out enough to make good firewood. Many country folks heat with firewood here in coal country. Life is good.

Vivian and Zeb look at their red and white barns. They painted the brown barns red and white soon after buying the farm. Those colors are just beautiful in their eyes on a barn. It warms their hearts to know that some wonderful orphans are in one barn and delightful farm animals in the other. They discuss the many improvements they have made and plans for future projects. What a life if you can get it.

Vivian notices the way the sun creates shadows on the barns. The red seems like a darker shade on the front of the barn than on the side with the sun's spotlight on it. The white is very bright in the sunlight.

They touch and hold hands some while rocking in the chairs. Vivian enjoys some cashews while Zeb has pecan pie. She tries to get him to cut down on sweets to no avail. She loves sunflower seeds from the Asian market too. They drive down to Harrisburg every couple weeks to stock up on Asian food. The Pho restaurant next to Highway 83 is the best down there.

Zeb is walking on the trails around the perimeter of the farm. He is smiling and chuckling that he and Vivian could buy this beautiful farm with cash. They worked hard for decades and were sitting on pile of dough and he is proud.

He looks up at the bright sun. The trees are about sixty feet tall. The sun rays are piercing through the branches and trunks. He cannot stop smiling at this paradise.

Zeb has some random thoughts. His mind races after consuming too much coffee. The thoughts are usually positive, but sometimes quite negative. The military will do that to you. You can fall back into seeing only threats and intentions and capabilities of possible enemies. He fights to stay positive and Christian and friendly.

"At least we should be okay if we have severe climate change. This farm is at 1,100 feet above sea level. It should take a while for the ocean to reach us. I guess this land used to be under the ocean anyway. The Earth has always had warming and cooling periods over billions of years. We will be gone if the ocean comes back to coal country," Zeb thinks to himself.

He thinks back to his father. He was drunk for thirty years and then died broke, dumb, and toothless. Zeb swore that he would never be like that. They say a man has two choices. First, he wants to be like his parents. Second, he rejects their values and lifestyle and wants to be nothing like his parents.

"Thank you God for Vivian and everything. Thank you for a great family and sweet friends and this awesome farm. No mortgage is the only way to go," Zeb says to himself walking on the trails he made.

He remembers his family and friends laughing at him for being careful with the money. Some of them spent too much on cars, vacations, and houses and went down in flames in foreclosure and bankruptcy. Vivian and Zeb have given a boatload of money and time to charity over the decades, but hate paying interest to the greedy bankers. They will never make the mistake of spending and borrowing too much.

Vivian is in the house cleaning. She is a bit of a germaphobe. She wears long and thick yellow gloves and a security grade N95 face mask. She sprays isopropyl alcohol all over the bathroom.

"How am I going to scrub behind the toilet seat? It is too tight back there. Why do they make it so small? Zeb is not very clean," Vivian thinks to herself.

She still smells the perfume from the neighbor from three months ago. Judy came by to borrow some sugar and her strong perfume smell lingers in the bathroom to this day. Judy plucked all her eyebrows and paints them on every day. She looks and drinks like an elderly Judy Garland.

Sometimes Zeb gets home and smells clorox from the garage. Vivian loves to clean and hounds Zeb to help. She shows him how dirty the swiffer is after cleaning the tile floor in the kitchen and hallways.

Vivian hates clutter. One time she had a yard sale while Zeb was on a trip to Daytona

Bike Week with some friends. She sold some of his old clothes and he was upset for a week after he returned. She threatens to have more yard sales if he buys too much stuff.

Zeb notices some animal footprints on the trails. He wonders if they are from deer or bears. Perhaps they are from foxes. The animals appreciate new trails when Zeb makes them. When he makes a new trail animal footprints always appear that night.

He sees a tree swaying in the wind. You can see straight through the trunk. The tree is dying from the inside. It is rotten all the way up to its forty foot peak. He wonders why he has never noticed this big tree before. It will fall soon. He hopes it falls away from his trail so he does not have to cut it with the chainsaw and drag it away.

He sees a vision of Vivian in his mind. She is so beautiful with thick black hair. Her Asian features are amazing with a spunky attitude included. He loves her very much and considers himself lucky to have such a farmer's wife. She jokes that he is no farmer. Is she cleaning the house again?

Vivian has seen the hard times in China and the United States. She will work hard to never go back to the dark times. She is an expert with Java software and at the top of her game. She loves Zeb and her family and friends. She never speaks without thinking.

Pat is like most people in rural America. They do not like big government, myopic politicians, and lazy people on welfare. He laughs at the redneck driving past the farm in his jacked up truck. 'EPA Evil' is on the big sticker on the truck's rear window. He is towing an ATV to the coal company's land to ride for fun. Many people ride dirt bikes and ATVs over in Saint Clair.

Pat drives his vehicle to the local one-man car repair business in Frackville. You can barely fit two cars into the bays and used parts line the walls. It is smoky inside the waiting room and a small TV is blasting a game show. It is three in the afternoon.

A large and cute old man is sitting and talking with another elderly customer. The mechanic shuffles around and looks like he could be the father of the two old customers. The cute and happy customer is wearing a thick, white cotton short-sleeve shirt with two breast pockets with two plastic shirt protectors full of pens. The shirt is too small and his huge stomach is sticking out. His jeans are too short and reveal his short white socks and little girl legs.

"Your car is so dirty. Why do you let it get so dirty? My wife would kill me if I did that. There is a good automatic car wash down in Ashland for $8 for the supreme wash. That is the one for me," the old man said.

"Well it is supposed to rain tomorrow," Pat replied.

"I better get back home. The wife does not let me eat out anymore. She says they put too much salt in the meat. Have a blessed day," the old man said.

"Do you mean that you have been out all day?" the other old man asks.

"Yes, I go out in the mornings and do not return until the afternoons. The wife would constantly get me to do stuff if I stayed home all day. That would really hurt my lifestyle. We used to work together all day at our pharmacy before we retired and that was tough let me tell you," the old man said.

Chapter Two
Greed- Ginger

"The problem of social organization is how to set up an arrangement under which greed will do the least harm, capitalism is that kind of a system," Milton Friedman. (2)

The Catholic Church has had 267 popes so far and some of them have not been quite up to standard if you know what I mean. Pope Boniface VIII was beaten to death in 1303 for seeking power and money with too much zest. (5)

May 2019
Ashland, PA

Ginger is twenty-two and tall and slender. She is the manager of the local wine and cheese store in the mall down in Saint Clair. She is very sweet, but has a tendency to take more than her share.

She used to horde diet cokes at the orphanage in her closet. Deep down she fears running out of stuff and food. This causes problems in her male relationships.

She often uses people for her own agenda. Many of her orphan friends do this as well. Ginger tries to overcome it, but many times fails at this. She has a big heart and tries to focus on God to make her a better person. She helps strangers all the time.

Her last boyfriend proclaimed that she had a sickness because she had one big cookie in her closet after he had told her he was starving late one night after work. That was the last straw for this young man.

Ginger forgot that she had a cookie for the hungry boyfriend. Later she rationalized the lack of food offer by thinking he should have planned ahead for his meals and snacks.

"How was your trip to New York City? I saw the weather forecast and it looked perfect," Pat asks.

"Well, we saw a man urinate on the sidewalk. I never saw that before. He was very dirty and relieved himself right there at the corner of Broadway and 40th," Ginger said.

"Wow, I bet that was funny. It looks like the fool would find a bathroom," Pat said.

"I know. Did I tell you that I saw a tractor trailer back door fly open and hit a Walmart tractor trailer down on Highway 61 in Pottsville the other day?" Ginger asks.

"Really? Those lanes are tight down there near Pizza Hut. The government folks need to fix the ruts in the asphalt too. That is dangerous for motorcycle riders. Did the Walmart driver see it happen?" Pat replies.

"Yes, he was gesticulating and yelling at the other driver, but he just kept on going. I do not think the driver who did not lock his rear door on the trailer even knew it happened," Ginger said.

"Those rear doors are huge. Do you know the middle name of that truck driver who lives over on Beaver Damn Road?" Pat said.

"No, is it something odd? He is a nice guy and gave us donuts the other day," Ginger said.

"His name is Dennis Ford Smith. How is that for a name? He told me that his father just really loved Ford vehicles and trucks," Pat said.

"That is quite an attachment to a brand. It is a good thing that the father did not love Renault or Toyota," Ginger said.

Zeb has Lynyrd Skynyrd cranked up in the barn. "Free Bird" from 1973 is entertaining the cows and horses.

Ginger had an incident at the Wine and Cheese corporate meeting last month. The owners have twenty stores and had a conference and meal at the Hershey Lodge. There was a thermos of coffee on a table for employees leaving for a two-hour excursion to the gardens.

Ginger filled up her thermos and walked out to the bus. Some of her co-workers saw her drain the container and they were left high and dry with no coffee for the bus trip. They now think she is too selfish or greedy.

She thought the container had plenty of coffee in it. She is too diffident to broach the subject with them. She is a hard worker and just makes mistakes like all of us. People can be so judgmental can't they?

"Did I tell you about the guy leaving a $20 tip the other day at the wine store?" Ginger asks.

"No, that is huge tip. How much wine did he buy? Perhaps he was trying to pick you up," Pat said.

"No, no he was just being generous after buying two bottles of white wine for $30. But my part-time worker thought we should split the tip for some reason. I said no way," Ginger said.

"Did she do anything to help with the sale?" Pat asks.

"No, she was not involved at all. Was I being greedy?" Ginger inquires.

"No, you did the right thing. That is good money. Do many customers leave tips?" Pat asks.

"No, it is pretty rare I must say. This guy always does and has a such a pleasant smile too. He says the people at Walmart do not know anything about wine," Ginger said.

Pat thinks to himself that maybe Ginger should have split the tip. Ginger is the manager after all and makes a lot more money than the part-timer. But his loyalty is to his sister and he keeps this thought to himself. Ginger is a hard worker and deserves to make a lot of money.

Vivian and Zeb are walking on their trails in the woods. They see about twenty fat, black animals in the distance. All of a sudden, these huge wild turkeys take off like jet airplanes. They cannot believe how fast they can fly with those huge torsos.

They love to walk the loop. Zeb cut down trees and brush all along the perimeter of the farm when they bought it. The trails are great for riding ATVs, dirt bikes, and go-karts for family and friends. Most days you can see deer running around and their foot prints in the soil or snow.

Zeb built a tree fort about fourteen feet above the ground for fun a while back. He and others climb the ladder to take in the awesome view of the tree, mountains, ponds, ducks, and geese. The tree fort sways in high winds between two trees that stand fifty feet tall. The deck is eight feet by eight feet and has no railing.

A guest asked Thomas Jefferson a long time ago at Monticello in Virginia once why he did not have a railing on his deck. Children may fall off and get hurt. TJ responded that it may be a good lesson for the kid. He loved the unobstructed view as does Zeb.

"Who was that on the phone? I cannot believe that those geese and ducks got out again," Ginger asks.

"That was Joe's daughter. She saw them on the road on her way to work," Pat said.

"Where are they getting out? We put chicken wire all around the pond, except on the pasture side," Ginger asks.

Every few days some of the birds get out of the pasture. They love to hang out on or near the country road. Many drivers come down the hill too fast and sometimes hit and kill them. The birds love to dig in the mud and water for food.

"Momo is so cute. He can fly, but mostly just walks with the geese all day. He is so beautiful with the green feathers," Ginger said.

"I know. He used to only hang with the Peking ducks, but he changed teams. It is sad that his entire mallard family is gone. I bet the hawks got them. He had six siblings and two parents in this pond last year," Pat said.

"Maybe the fisher cats got them. I saw those disgusting things running across the road a few months ago, Ginger said.

It is a battle during the warm months to protect the birds from prey. Huge hawks circle overhead looking for a meal. Fisher cats live across the road sometimes. There are foxes and coyote around too.

"I saw that guy you embarrassed on Valentine's Day in Saint Clair today. You are the queen of revenge," Pat said.

"Hey, he had it coming to him. He would always ensure that he took better care of himself than me. If I had the six ounce sirloin, he would get the ten ounce. It is a sickness Pat," Ginger said.

"True, but did you not take a picture of his expensive boots he bought for himself and put them on Facebook?" Pat asks.

"I sure did. He forgot to get me anything for Valentine's Day and bought those expensive boots for himself. Revenge is a very good quality. Haha," Ginger said.

"That was awesome. Who is he to buy the best for himself? Who is he to look after number one?" Pat asks.

"Yes, you are correct. But what about you and the picker from Penn State?" Ginger asks.

"Oh, yes the picker. I have not thought about her in a while. She picked that nose all the time. It was traumatizing. She said she had a medical condition," Pat said.

"She was creative to blame the bad habit on a medical condition. Maybe she thought that would shield her from criticism. She could name it Acute Pickophilia or Nasal Debris Diversion Disorder," Ginger said.

"Okay, that is enough. This conversation reminds me of eighth grade. We have officially hit rock bottom. I just wonder what she was doing with all that gold she dug up," Pat said.

A white truck pulls up to the barn. It is huge with a walk-in cover on the bed of the truck with refrigeration. Ginger and Pat greet the driver.

"Hello! Is Timmy here?" the driver asks.

"No Timmy lives here. Vivian and Zeb own the place and they are not home right now," Ginger answers.

"Oh, okay. I guess Timmy sold them the farm a while back. I have not stopped by here in years," driver.

"What is in your truck? It looks very sophisticated," Pat asks.

"This specialized truck is very expensive. We sell bull sperm to ranchers who breed cows," the driver said.

"Wow, I have never heard of that product. I can take your number and give it to Zeb," Pat said.

The driver leaves with the truck full of sperm. Ginger and Pat discuss this odd bull sperm salesman situation.

"I wonder what his parents say about him to the neighbors. My son is a good boy. He rides around selling bull sperm. It is a growing field. He always has plenty of sperm. Yes, he is a good boy; very successful," Ginger said.

"Yes, my boy has the highest quality bull sperm this side of the Mississippi River. He only settles for the best sperm. This stuff is potent. These are fast swimmers. You should see the cows that this stuff produces. It is radioactive," Pat said.

Ginger and Pat drive down to Saint Clair to the Italian restaurant for lunch. The kitchen has a coal oven that burns twice as hot as wood. The pizza is to die for and everything has been delicious in their previous visits.

"Aw, this turkey wrap is terrible. I think they put too much mustard on here. I cannot finish this. The wrap is soggy," Ginger said.

"Really? That is amazing. Everything we have ever had here has been great. The peanut butter pie is unbelievable. I love the sausage, pepperoni, and mushroom pizza pie," Pat said.

The server comes by to check on them. The place is packed and the service is a little slow today. There is a guy on stage in the corner reading from his book. He wrote a humor book and attempting to entertain the folks and perhaps sell some books.

"How is everything?" the server asks.

"Good, everything is good," Ginger and Pat say in unison as the server brushes past on the way to other tables.

Their instincts just kick in to be nice and noncontroversial at all times. That is just the way they were brought up at the orphanage. They do not like to start arguments or fights. They laugh about their little white lie after the server leaves the table.

"Why did we say that? This wrap is awful. I just cannot complain because we get that server sometimes and usually the food is great," Ginger said.

"It is odd that we cannot manage the speak the truth to help them improve their food. Let us just go with the lie. We are the freaks now," Pat said.

"That guy on stage is Easy Eddie. He wrote some funny books on Amazon. I bought the first one and it was pretty good, but nothing to write home about. Let me get these mints over here before we leave," Ginger said.

Ginger walks around the booth and grabs many mints from the other tables and on the counter. She dumps them into her purse and always wants more than she gets. She chalks it up to human nature to avoid introspection.

"Do not let them see you do that. You cannot embarrass the family. I will buy you some at Walmart. You are nuts," Pat jokes.

Pat is looking at himself in the mirror. He loves the way his hair flows and his strong chin. He has always thought he was glorious and impressive. He tries to see if he has food between his teeth.

"Do not look too long. You will break the mirror. You look like a gorilla," Ginger jokes as she catches him admiring himself a little too long.

The orphans like to rib each other all the time. Their weaknesses and strengths are fair game with their biting comments and jokes. The more brutal the better with this bunch.

Ginger and Pat leave a big tip even though the service was slow. The place was packed with customers. It does not matter that the turkey wrap tasted bad. All the food at this restaurant was great before. They understand imperfection and give the server a great tip. They know what it is like to have a bad day and have mercy on the server.

Ginger thinks about the boundaries and pearls of wisdom in the Bible. They have kept her safe and successful her entire life. She loves God, Jesus, family, and friends. Nobody is perfect and that keeps life very interesting.

"As long as I follow the New Testament, everything will be fine. We will have ups and downs and that is fine. God help me to follow you until the end of time," Ginger says to herself.

They drive through the village of Shenandoah. They see a huge billboard on the side of the bumpy and patched country road. The politicians and government employees waste so much money on dumb programs that they cannot pave the roads. They even leave the Christmas decorations up year round to save money.

The billboard says "Everybody's Goal is to Mine More Coal."

Ginger and Pat laugh about the suggestion to maintain and create more dangerous and low paying jobs. The local people believe any job is a good job. Perhaps they can make the jobs safer and higher paying. The greedy politicians and business owners cannot do that.

They notice the small houses on the road. Many have moss or fungus on the siding. There are houses with green and blue metal siding that is falling off the house. Many people are barely getting by here.

Ginger sees three cats in a window. She thinks they are cardboard cutouts that are painted black and gray. Two of them start to move and walk around on the window sill and she realizes that all three are real and alive. The house is rotting and it looks vacant. She says a prayer for the residents to herself.

Pat starts singing a song about the village motto on the billboard. He creates the song kind of like a children's tale. "To mine more coal is our only goal. We have one goal and that to mine more coal. The coal, coal, coal is our only goal, goal, goal," he goes on an on.

"How many times do people make suggestions that can be interpreted as good and bad at the same time? I remember my friend was joking around and suggested that her mother with a bad temper get a boyfriend," Ginger said.

"Did she suggest that so the old woman would release the sexual tension and be more relaxed and nice?" Pat said.

"Yes, and so the argumentative old woman would be nicer to those around her including her husband. Everyone walked on egg shells around this unpleasant woman," Ginger said.

"Oh, okay. I guess our judgment of whether a suggestion is good or bad depends on the time frame you are examining. Do you want good results now or in the future?" Pat asks.

"Yes, I had a boss one time that only cared about how his decisions affected the company while he was in charge. He did not care if things fell apart after his evaluation period and when he left that position," Ginger said.

"Many politicians are like that and only care about getting elected to a higher position. They will always try to cover up stuff and their mistakes until after the election. Myopia is the way for dumb folks," Pat said.

Back at the barn Vivian and Zeb are feeding the pigs. There are ten of them in a small shed or shelter near one of the huge barns. The shed opens to a twenty by twenty foot pen. There are two adults and eight baby pigs and they are fun to watch.

The babies are doing circles and running around the pen. They stop briefly to eat and drink. They look like cars going around a track. The mother pig is playing with a big rubber ball. She is trying to bite it and spinning around with it.

The father is taking it easy and just eating. He watches the babies and the humans.

The babies roll over on the ground and jump back up and run around like they are crazy. Their tails are wagging and they seem to be smiling.

They munch on hay and alfalfa. They get apples and raisins as treats sometimes. The pigs will eat just about anything you throw their way.

"You know you look like that when you eat. What do you like to eat? Do you think you eat too much? Maybe you have the pig gene," Vivian jokes.

"You are so funny. You should be a comedian. Well, I do love to eat. Let us go to the Japanese steak house in Saint Clair for lunch. Hibachi steak is calling my name. This is making me hungry for sure," Zeb replies.

"I remember we had a team leader from Germany four our IT group. He took us out for lunch in Harrisburg to this barbecue place. He was overweight and licked his fingers so much after he ate two plates of ribs. It was so funny," Vivian said.

"I imagine that he looked like a big pig. I bet people ran when he tried to shake their hand. All leaders need to appoint someone to follow them around and tell them when they are doing bad or weird things. The world would be a better place," Zeb said.

"He was funny. He kept saying that we need to take it to a higher level. Nobody knows what that means. The German was trying to motivate us. You know he got laid off a couple months after that," Vivian said.

"I remember meeting his assistant who wore the low cut tops and thick makeup. She was a yes woman and sucking up to him all the time. I guess that was her idea to go out to eat with the team for his birthday," Zeb said.

"He may have been fired because he locked that guy out one morning when he came to work and told everyone to ignore him knocking on the office door and windows. There was just something off with respect to that firing. He called the police instead of the security guard and just stood there laughing at the poor unemployed guy trying to get back in to clear out his desk," Vivian said.

"I bet the fired guy was freaking out. I wonder why they fired him. That situation seems a bit unprofessional, but maybe the guy did something horrible," Zeb said.

"The German guy brought his sexy Russian girlfriend to the company dinner. She wore a red short and tight dress and five inch heels. His pants and suits were always too small for his body. They were drinking a lot that night.

I wonder is she left him after the money ran out," Vivian said.

"I remember you said the yes woman got promoted after that. And then she quit under pressure from some scandal. She smoked cigarettes like wild when we saw her in your parking lot," Zeb said.

"Yes, she was promoted to team leader and then it was obvious to all that she did not know what she was doing. She was not qualified to lead anybody. She asked the dumbest questions at our meetings for a couple weeks and then quit," Vivian said.

"That guy had a nice Mercedes Benz. That was top of the line. I loved the fat tires. I wonder if it was a lease car. Many people lease cars to put on a big show without actually having money. Most leases are a rip off," Zeb said.

"How did you know that? He asked us if anyone wanted to take over his lease payments when they fired him. He said money was tight and he was moving back to Germany to look for a job," Vivian said.

"That is why I am so glad that we pay cash for everything. Cash is king on this farm. We hate paying interest. We only paid $400 interest last year," Zeb said.

"That is your fault. I still do not understand why you bought that new motorcycle. It looks like the other one," Vivian said.

"My newer 2018 Harley-Davidson Breakout has more technology and is thirty pounds lighter than the previous year's model. It is better for older guys like me and not as easy to drop. The engine is awesome with four spark plugs and massive horsepower. I love the chrome turbine wheels. I deserve the best," Zeb said.

"So? You do not deserve the best. Let us pay no interest this year. How about that? That is the last Harley for you. I am going to get some work done next year," Vivian jokes.

Vivian is always joking about getting some plastic surgery. She is beautiful with smooth skin, but knows some women who get work done to remove the wrinkles. She tells Zeb that it is too late for him to improve his looks.

Ginger and Bruce are chatting on the deck of the barn. It is on a foggy spring morning. The steam is rising off the trees on the beautiful mountains. Many clouds are blowing over the farm with patches of blue sky.

Ginger has always been infatuated with money and riches. People tell her over and over that money does not buy happiness, but she thinks they are wrong. She thinks about a book she read about Houdini and when he got rich and famous. He was so joyful when he gave gold coins to his mother. (9)

"Did I tell you about what Harry Houdini did? I was just thinking about that book I read about him. He was quite the entertainer," Ginger said.

"No, I have heard of him, but do not know anything except that he was a famous magician. I think they wrote over five hundred books about him for some reason," Bruce said.

"His father was an out of work rabbi dying and asked that he always take care of his mother. Much later Houdini demanded that one employer pay him in gold coins. He then took the sack of coins and asked his mother to hold out her apron. He then poured the coins into his mother's apron," Ginger said.

"Why do you like that story so much? I bet you would like a sack of gold coins to play with. You know love is more important than money," Bruce said.

"I can just imagine how fun that was to be rich and drop gold coins in your mother's apron. He must have been so proud of his success and money. I bet his mother loved it," Ginger said.

"You are crazy. But I bet the mother was so proud to have such a successful son. I wonder if our mothers would be proud of us," Bruce said.

"That would be great to know. You know in 1926 a college student was playing around and punched Houdini in the abdomen a couple times and then the next day he died from peritonitis and a ruptured appendix at age 52. How about that for an ending?" Ginger said.

"Boy, what a dumb way to die. Imagine having all that success and money and then allowing a college student to punch you like idiots on spring break in Florida," Bruce said.

The fog and clouds lift to reveal a bright blue sky. The green trees are waving in the breeze. The mountains seem to rise up toward the sky. They enjoy the vista, cheesecake, and coffee in the Adirondack chairs on the deck.

"Do you know one thing I will never understand? Some people believe that all this is unplanned. They believe that this awesome planet, all the animals, and even humans all are here by chance. It is so sad that they do not believe in God and Jesus as we do," Ginger said.

"I am with you. There is no way in my mind that this is an accident. God created all this and it could not occur by happenstance. God and Jesus are great! I pray for the believers and non-believers," Bruce said.

"I thank God for you and everything good in this fallen world. We will be fine if we follow the Bible and God. That is what we know for sure. That Bible is worth its weight in gold," Ginger said.

Vivian brought a huge cheesecake to the barn this morning for the orphans. The breeze feels so good on the deck. They are like two siblings catching up after being separated for a few months. All the bills are paid. Life is good on the farm.

Zeb is mowing the grass on the zero turn John Deere. He loves his grass mowing machine. All of a sudden, he turns the mower off and runs over the Bruce's vehicle. He thoroughly cleans the chrome wheels and tires on the vehicle. He does this to make them laugh up on the deck.

Bruce is fanatical about keeping his wheels clean and lathering tire wet on his tires to keep them shiny black. He goes into overdrive the minute the rain stops to keep his vehicle spotless. Zeb ribs him for this obsession.

The grass smells good after the mowing. It is very green and the lawn is huge at three acres. Vivian and Zeb love wide open spaces so much. The squirrels are running around and digging and looking for nuts and other food. Zeb mows the grass more often than necessary and never complains about having a big yard. Vivian reads the news on the upper deck of their house. She chews on sunflower seeds and enjoys her farm and family.

Ginger takes a walk over to Beaver Damn Road. She walks by the Manning house. It is falling down and nobody has lived there in a long time. They story is that a couple lived there and fought all the time. They yelled at anyone who approached the house.

The old guy was a laid off coal miner and drank a lot. He was obese with a long, gray beard. There was never any love in the house.

It is kind of like that song by Tom Waits "House Where Nobody Lives." He has so many great songs like "Make It Rain."

The house is made of cheap formaldehyde siding with thick, green moss growing on it. Vines are growing all over the roof and the rusted gutters. An old sign in the window says "Leave Me Alone." The old guy had a sense of humor until the end.

Ginger has heard all the stories from neighbors about this anti-social couple. They both died in a car wreck many years ago. Ginger says a prayer for the couple and all the elderly people. She volunteers to feed them sometimes at the church in Ashland with her friend Ann Marie. A hard life can turn your heart cold.

The old guy shot the neighbor's dog with his hunting rifle one time. The old woman called the police on the neighbor for attracting flies, gnats, and mosquitoes with a fish tank. Ginger wonders how they got that mean and anti-social. She has some questions.

"Did they love anyone? Did they have children? Did they suffer for their sins? Were they just misunderstood? Did Jehovah's

Witnesses stop by to visit? Did the old guy take off his shirt to freak them out? Why don't they tear down the dilapidated house?" Ginger asks herself.

Someone told her that he took off his shirt and shook his belly at people just to get a reaction. The old guy used to urinate on his bushes in the front yard.

Ginger thanks God and Jesus for her loving family and friends at the barn. They would never act like the old and nasty couple over here on Beaver Damn Road. She believes that the Bible provides some great rules for life. They explain boundaries for good and bad behavior. She loves to read and re-read the New Testament for daily living advice.

Donald and Zeb ride by on their motorcycles and give the thumbs up. The Harley-Davidsons growl and shake the road. Ginger bows down in honor to give them fake praise for comedic effect. She dated a guy one time who loved his Harley more than her. He would buy stuff all the time for the bike and claim to be broke to her. Things just did not work out with that jackass.

All of a sudden, a fox dances across the country road with a baby in her mouth. These animals are shy and Ginger only sees them about once a year. The mother is rust colored, thin, and small. This makes Ginger's day and she smiles all the way back to the barn. You are not going to see a fox living in dirty and polluted Philadelphia.

It just stopped raining and the birds are singing in the trees. The tiny birds are flying all around. They chase each other in the wind. Rain droplets fall from the tree branches onto the dirt, grass, and road. Ginger soaks up this rural landscape and is so glad she does not live in the big city filled with smells of urine, body odor, and trash.

Ginger thinks about the city kid who visited a couple weeks ago. He was a cousin of the neighbor. He was always on his cellphone playing games and on social media. This behavior is odd out here in rural America. People look down on it.

Most of the people here think it is dumb to play on a phone all the time. Many are aware of research that it can lead to anxiety and depression. The Earth and all upon it are much more interesting than being on a phone all the time. Ginger suggested that he get off the phone and enjoy the real world. She showed the Boston kid the tree fort, crossbow, and minibike and he loved them.

Ginger examines all the odd mailboxes beside the country road. There is the fish mailbox. The mouth is a circular door for the postal worker. There are several John Deere mailboxes that look like tractors and mowers. One mailbox has 'No More Bullshit- Vote for Trump' on it. Another box looks like a big golf ball.

The old postal worker for this route lost a tooth last week and had to postpone the delivery. She has long gray hair and always cheerful in leggings. Her boss delivered the mail that night. They work hard in the post office in Ashland. They bend the rules for their customers the way they never would in the big city.

The only bad thing is the roads in Ashland. You could lose a pet in the potholes. There is asphalt patch upon asphalt patch. There are orange circles drawn around the potholes from years ago by the workers who never came back to fill them. The village budget is tight with so many unemployed folks.

The old biker always sits on the bench. His dog wears sunglasses. The man speaks fast and most people cannot understand him. He is very friendly and loves for people to take his picture with the dog. He was laid off many years ago from a small coal mine.

There are weird businesses in Ashland. One guy sells used golf balls and furniture. Another sells beads and string. The woman on the corner sells new and used dolls. Most of them are very old and faded. Business is a little slow right now.

A redneck rides by in his jacked up Chevrolet pickup with fat tires. He has two chrome stickers on the rear window. Ginger enjoys seeing funny bumper stickers and window stickers. She saw one last week that said, "Vietnam Veteran: Leave Me Alone."

This guy today has two silhouettes of a well endowed woman in a bikini or nude with long hair. She is sitting on grass or perhaps dirt. One sticker is on the lower left window and the other on the lower right window. One of them has a devil's tail and the other an angel's halo. Ginger wonders what kind of nut buys and displays these stickers. Isn't one enough?

The Triumph song "Lay It On The Line" is blaring out the windows. The bass, drums, and guitar are vibrating the truck and road. The redneck is playing air drums and driving at the same time. He enjoys a cigar also.

Chapter Three
Lust- Tammy

"The more we are filled with thoughts of lust, the less we find true romantic love," Douglas Horton. (2)

Tammy and Billy are walking from the barn to the pond on a Saturday morning. She cooked pancakes and sausage for them on this day off from work and college. All of a sudden fifty Canadian geese fly in circles above the pasture and then land in the pond. Tammy gets a great video of the impressive arrival.

She is twenty-three and he is twenty years old. Her hair is long and blond and her shape is like that of an Olympic gymnast. The men love the way the walks and talks. They cannot get enough.

Tammy and this guy have been dating for two months and it is going well. They met at the Lutheran Church and hit it off by talking about history.

"Wow, I have never seen a group of birds do that!" Billy said.

"This group has been flying in for two weeks now. They stay for the day and then fly out in the afternoon," Tammy said.

Tammy's phone vibrates and a text comes in. She pulls it out of her pocket and somehow Billy sees the message.

"Hey baby. Do you look hot today?" the text message states.

"Who is that? I cannot believe you are cheating on me already!" Billy said.

"It is just some guy from school. He likes to talk trash," Tammy explains.

Billy storms off and leaves the farm forever. He will not take anyone cheating on him. The sad thing is that Billy is a much better catch or man than the flirtatious guy from the college.

The frisky guy touched Tammy in the cafeteria the other day and she let the lust control her. This guy only wants one thing and has a dark heart. She is being punished for her bout of intense desire.

"In my experience lust only ever leads to misery," Chrissie Hynde, Lead Singer of The Pretenders. (2)

Zeb and Vivian are in their house reading the news in the Wall Street Journal and online. The flock of Canadian geese circle and land in the front yard. She is upstairs in the bed reading and he is downstairs at the breakfast table.

"Come see! Quick come see this!" Vivian yells to Zeb downstairs.

They both run out onto the upper porch of the house to see all the geese walking around in the yard. They are huge and beautiful. Some are flapping their wings and talking to each other.

"Wow! That is amazing. There must be fifty of them walking around in our front yard. This place is paradise for sure," Zeb said.

They hear "Green River" by Creedence Clearwater Revival (CCR) coming from the barn. Vivian is the rare person here in coal country who dislikes rock and roll music. She calls it monkey music because many singers scream and the fans crank it up very loud. Zeb just smiles and enjoys the day.

Tammy works in the bookstore at Penn State's campus in Schuylkill Haven down Highway 61. She always wears a smile on her pretty face and is very dependable. She is earning a bachelor's degree in business and studies hard.

A few months ago she got into trouble at work. She kissed a guy in the bookstore one day after a date. Her boss saw this display of unprofessional behavior and let her have it.

"We must have boundaries at work. You cannot touch or kiss anyone while you are representing this bookstore. Please be professional," Tom, the manager gently explains.

Tammy will figure it out. She is smart and reads the Bible sometimes. Many people struggle with self-control and self-discipline.

Zeb always suggests the local auto repair shop to his renters. He knows the owner Tim and they have a secret arrangement. Tim gives the renters a low bill for parts and service and Zeb pays 30% on the side. This helps the youngsters in the barn save a ton of money on vehicle maintenance and repairs.

Tammy had an expensive car breakdown last year and Zeb saved her $1,800. He thinks this is the best way to help them be self sufficient, confident, Christian, and strong. Money is tight for most youngsters trying to make their way in this world. Zeb teaches them to work hard, avoid paying much interest on loans, read books and articles, and save for retirement. Vivian and Zeb love these kids in the barn and thank God for them every day.

"Is that a car flipped over? Oh my God I think it is! I am calling 911," Tammy said.

"I thought I saw something, but I cannot believe that is a car. They must have just wiped out," Bruce said.

Tammy and Bruce are driving back to the barn from the Redner's grocery store in Shenandoah. They spot an overturned car beside Highway 61. The lights are on and the wheels are still spinning. It is just past dusk and getting darker. There are many trees and rocks on the hillside next to the highway.

"Help! Help! Get me out! Help me please!" the man in the car yells for help.

"It is okay. It is okay. We called 911 and the police and rescue squad are on the way. Just take it easy. Try to stay still," Tammy tells the driver.

"Get me out! Please help me out! I cannot stay in here. My leg is hurt. My foot is trapped," the driver yells.

After the pleading for help to get out of the smashed car, Bruce pulls the driver out the rear window. He has cuts on his arms and head, but otherwise looks okay.

"It is amazing that you are okay! That car is really messed up. You are so lucky!" Tammy said.

Bruce sees pills all over the dirt and a vodka bottle inside the car. Tammy recognizes the opioids on the ground and sees a couple pill bottles. Several trees are ripped up and they hear a motor running in the car. They help the guy walk away from the car in case it explodes.

A policeman comes and asks the guy some questions.

"Are you legal to drive?" the cop asks the driver.

"I had my license, but it was revoked for a fine and DUI," the driver explains.

The driver has a mo-hawk haircut and many tattoos. He smells like alcohol and seems very nervous.

"Boy, that was wild! I cannot believe he flipped the car over. How did he do that? He must have been flying," Tammy said.

"I know, that is crazy. The opioid epidemic is for real. That guy is in big trouble now with the heat. Thank God he did not get hurt or die," Bruce said.

They drive home and thank God for the man's safety and that they are not on drugs or alcohol. Coal country is full of people on welfare and drugs.

Tammy used to volunteer with the Red Cross during blood drives. Somehow over time she developed a fear of needles and now cannot get near them. She panics when she has to give blood for physicals nowadays.

"I wonder why you are so repulsed by needles now after all those years being around them. You used to give blood all the time," Bruce said.

"I do not know what happened. I think part of it is that a hospital used to have a program where you could give blood for future use by a family member or friend. I gave for the old secretary at the school," Tammy said.

"You are so sweet. I remember she was sickly, poor, and without good health insurance. I guess if she ever needed blood, it was free because you gave in her name," Bruce said.

Tammy goes to bed a little early because she is bored with the content on all the channels. She awakens at two in the morning worried about something that will never happen to her. She has an irrational fear of becoming addicted to drugs.

She is very firm in her life against taking legal or illegal drugs. She has seen her share of friends who struggled with the problem.

Tammy loves men and thinks perhaps it is because everyone must have a vice to deal with. Nobody is perfect. She tries to go by the Bible which preaches moderation. When she needs prescription drugs, she will never take the entire number suggested by the doctor. She views the doctors as drug dealers who must be punished when they give drugs to addicts like candy.

She thinks back to college and the time she secretly dated twins. The scheme only lasted one week when the twins realized the scheme. Tammy wanted to see how similar or different the identical twins were.

The twins became angry with her when they realized that she had no interest in them other than for some weird experiment. They think she is a very cold and calculating person. Tammy is very generous with her time and money. She just struggles with loving the opposite sex way too much. Men are so very interesting to her. She must discover everything about them. It is kind of creepy for the men in her life.

She views her pursuit of twins as a victimless crime. She is just having fun as a young American. Tammy's dates are usually impressed with her looks, conversation, and spirit. She loves to explore and have a good time.

She has not found triplets yet, but will some day. What makes them tick? How are they similar and dissimilar? How are their views of their parents different? Their realities must be different in their own minds even though they grew up in the same reality.

Tammy's weakness is lust or the intense desire for men, love, affection, and power. She does not go all the way with most men, but always really enjoys the affection. She tries to substitute the desire with eating great food, but it is just not the same. Tammy always reverts back to seeking and spending time with the men.

She prays to God every day to allow her self control and to be a normal person. She does a lot of good in life, but knows she desires men a little too much.

The wind is blowing very hard on the farm. It blew some chairs off the deck of the barn. Tammy hears a big tree crack and fall down in the forest behind the barn. The windows are straining to stay firm and keep the wind out.

She feels guilty about her lust for men. Tammy will double her gift to the Muscular Dystrophy organization when she gets paid. Maybe she will send more to the National Multiple Sclerosis Society too.

Tammy ruminates about how all humans are capable of such good things and evil things. She mostly prevents the bad things by following the teachings of Jesus in the New Testament of The Bible. That gives her boundaries to never cross. She is strong and a great person. Any man would be so lucky to have her.

She thinks she hears a squirrel running around above her apartment. Perhaps it is a bird scampering around up there. The toilet flushes in the bathroom she shares with men and women. Tammy hopes it is a clean woman and not a not-so-clean man.

She loves men, but is well aware that many of them have trouble with cleanliness inside and out of the restroom. Many emit foul odors at all times of the day and have too much hair sticking out. Perhaps the caveman still roams the Earth.

Tammy thinks back to dating that guy from Bloomsburg. He looked and acted like a Neanderthal with a sloping and protruding forehead, flat skull, and reduced chin. That relationship was doomed from the start.

He was kind of dumb and reinforced her history books that described how they could not compete the modern humans about 40,000 years ago in Europe and became extinct.

The Neanderthal was the lead singer in a local rock band. The band members lacked talent, but she thought it would be exciting dating a band member. For their first date, he said that his car is broken and asked if she could pick him up at his apartment and go out to eat.

She gets to the nice, small house in an older neighborhood in Gordon. He is nowhere to be found. She calls his cellphone and he directs her to this apartment.

She walks beside the normal tiny house down the driveway to a two-story garage in the back yard. A broken down car is in the driveway. It has dents all over, flat tires, and will never run again. His dirty apartment is upstairs.

He finally appears and invites her in for the meal. He serves up canned beans and discount soda from the Boyer's grocery store. She quickly discovers that this is the meal and he is dirt poor. There will be no meal at a nice restaurant. Worse than that is the fact that he has no musical talent or job skills and no prospects. This is their first and only date.

Tammy grins and laughs about her only date with a rock and roll musician. The lesson she learns is to never again involve herself with a rock musician with bad credit. She avoids all men with protruding foreheads also. She finally falls back to sleep at 3:30 in the morning.

Vivian and Zeb built the apartments upstairs in the barn where hay would be stored if they had animals in this barn. There is basically a rectangular box within the walls of the barn which comprise seven apartments and two bathrooms. There are open walkways on one side of the box.

They have a great room with a big TV, stereo, sofa, chairs, and a dart board at the end of the box. Vivian and Zeb provide a lot of extras for these special guests. The orphans add so much to their lives at the farm.

The farm owners and the renters are much more than landlords and tenants. It is a family unit full of love and respect and an oasis to the cruel world around them. There is never any violence or horrible behavior here because Vivian and Zeb would never allow it.

The orphans are protected and loved as children are in the best of Christian homes. They know co-workers who describe greedy and abusive landlords who are just plain nasty to speak with. Perhaps the cliche is true that money is the root of all evil.

Their friends at work tell them how old and ugly male landlords actually try to date their young and attractive tenants. Sometimes the gross apartment owners try over and over like predators. They laugh it off and joke about telling their wives how dumb they really are.

One guy constantly asks the pretty women to go boating with him. His breath is draconian and his teeth in bad shape. He apparently has a fishing boat on the Susquehanna River and a fishing cabin. This overweight man tries and fails to corral the young beauties all the time.

They view him as the Harvey Weinstein of Ashland. Many men try to leverage their positions to gain access to beautiful women. God help the youngsters be strong and Christian. They are the future and must be nurtured, educated, and promoted. Love will rule the day in a Christian and capitalistic society such as the United States of America.

"Our Constitution was made only for a moral and religious people. It is wholly inadequate to the government of any other," President John Adams. (2)

Tammy drives down to Frackville to get a take-out pizza. The place is on Main Street. There are deep potholes all along the road and the row houses look like they are falling down. Coal country has seen its better days.

She sits on a bench outside while the pie is cooking. The restaurant burns coal in the oven. An old man is sitting on the other bench and strikes up a conversation. The Holy Ascension Orthodox Church is across the street with its gorgeous gold domes.

"What kind of pizza pie are you getting? My wife and I like pepperoni and sausage with mushrooms," the old man asks.

"We are getting chicken and black olives on ours. Sometimes we get what you are getting. Where you in the Air Force? I see your cap," Tammy said.

"Yes, I was stationed in Pakistan back in the 1960s. Francis Powers was stationed there before me flying for the CIA. The communist Russians shot him down in 1960," the old man explains.

"Really? I remember something about that from history class. Did he die?" Tammy asks.

"No, he was flying at 70,000 feet so the Soviets could not reach him. But the US intelligence folks were wrong and they shot him down. He parachuted to the ground and decided not to commit suicide with his poison pill," the old man explains.

"Wow, it is amazing that he lived at that altitude. I guess you need oxygen above 12,000 feet. Was your wife in the military too?" Tammy asks.

"No, we were both pharmacists in Shenandoah. We are retired now and met in Philadelphia," the old man said.

"Really? How did you meet? I love to ask old people that. Sorry, I love to ask anyone that question," Tammy asks.

"No offense taken. I was a senior in pharmacy school and saw this beautiful freshman. I helped her with directions one day. After that meeting, I was obsessed with her," the old man explains.

"Wow, that is romantic. I guess you have been married a long time. You must live around here too. I live in Ashland and rent from the Browns," Tammy said.

"Yes, we have always just clicked. I cannot imagine being with someone else. I am fascinated with people who never get married. I could not do that," the old man said.

"I agree, someday I will get married. I just need to find the right man. This woman I work with has a brother who never got married," Tammy said.

"Really? I wonder why he never married. It would be so lonely for me. I could never do that," the old man said.

"He never married because he saw his parents fight and yell all the time. There was not much love between his parents. He never connected with anyone enough to get married. He is gay now," Tammy said.

"That is interesting. It looks like he would marry a man in that situation. He must be very independent and enjoy solitude. I guess many couples argue a lot and should probably part ways," the old man said.

"Has this village always looked this bad? I see potholes, old bathtubs, and broken down row houses here. It must have been nicer many years ago. Look at the cracked sidewalks and mold on the houses," Tammy asks.

"This place peaked with about 8,000 residents in the 1940s. It went downhill when the coal mines closed during the last few decades. I guess about 4,000 folks live here now," the old man said.

"My friend told me that the Frackville mall closed in 2017. That warehouse is huge they built on that site," Tammy said.

"Yes, that is a shame that the mall shut down. We used to walk there in the winter. This village used to have a recording studio and brewery believe it or not," the old man said.

"Really? I cannot believe that. It looks like someone would open a tour business here just to see Centralia. That is interesting history with the coal mine fires over there," Tammy said.

Their pizzas come out and they part ways. Tammy notices a brick wall separating from the front of a row house as she walks to her car. The brick wall is about five feet high in front of some cracked stairs. It is about five inches from the block wall behind the brick and leaning toward the sidewalk.

A local policeman is handcuffing a drunk guy in front of the falling brick wall. He is about thirty years old and bald with many tattoos. He is not wearing a shirt. His grammar is terrible and his speech is slurred. A broken whiskey bottle is at his feet. He is a loud fellow.

"This place has gone down hill for sure. Why do these less than desirable folks stand out for attention? Where are the kind and Christian citizens?" Tammy says to herself.

An old lady approaches Tammy while passing on the sidewalk. She is smiling and very well dressed. She notices something about Tammy and very interested in speaking with her. This much is obvious.

"Excuse me. I love your outfit. Do you mind telling me where we can buy it? I will tell my granddaughter about it. You look very cute in that outfit! Have a blessed day and enjoy being young. You look like pretty flowers on a bright spring day," the old lady said.

"I guess I spoke too soon. That lady is so nice! I wish all people were as nice as her. Do not be so negative," Tammy says to herself.

Tammy notices an old house with rusted metal siding on it. A big rotten tree fell down on the porch and into a front window on the second floor. The house looks abandoned and she wonders why nobody removed the tree or repaired the house. Does anyone live there? The roof is sagging under the weight of the tree and must leak a lot.

She sees the silhouette of a man upstairs staring out the broken window and suddenly looks away. The answer is that someone does live in this broken down house. Money must be tight.

"I wonder if he is a down and out coal miner. Does he live alone? Perhaps he is a drug addict? God and Jesus please help the downtrodden. Thank you for everything. Please help my family and friends. Please let us never end up like that," Tammy says to herself.

She thinks about the old man in the window and asks herself several questions. How do people end up like that? Do they make one horrible decision or many terrible choices? Is he married? Did he ever marry? What does he do all day? Did he work hard like me? Was he lazy when he was young? Did he ever help other folks?

Tammy gets back to her apartment in the barn and writes and mails checks to several charities. She is so thankful to have extra money and great friends. Checks go out to the Muscular Dystrophy Association, The American Red Cross, Our Daily Bread, Make a Wish, and St. Judes Children's Hospital.

Tammy thinks back to the old finance professor in college. He used to wale for hours about saving for retirement. He was old and wise. His jokes were not very good. His shirts and pants were always very wrinkled.

"It is not how much you make, but how much you save. Ensure that you have at least $4,000 coming in each month for doing nothing or sitting on your porch. We must prepare for when we are tired or sick and old. Work hard when you are young and have plenty of energy. Read the books. Do not be lazy! I have many toothless friends and family who never learned or ignored this advice," Professor Weaver would say.

Tammy made friends with Latrice. She was blind from birth and was an orphan too. They took a Personal Finance class together and really enjoyed it. They used to study together in the library. Latrice scored higher on all the tests than the lazy students with perfect vision. This inspired Tammy to study harder and read all the books she could get her hands on.

Latrice is African American and very short. She always has a smile on her face and can play piano like a professional musician. She grew up in Wilmington, NC with foster parents. She is very Christian and friendly to everyone. Her voice is like an angel and she sang in the choir as a child.

Tammy and Latrice still stay in touch and will get together again at some point, but it is a long way from Pennsylvania to North Carolina. They used to laugh about the cartoon drawing in Dr. Weaver's office. They will always remember the clothes balled up in the corner of his tiny office. Books and papers were thrown everywhere.

The cartoon is huge. It measures about three feet by two feet. It shows a bum sitting on the curb. He has only one shoe on with holes in his socks. He is reading the Wall Street Journal. He has a serious expression on his unshaven face.

"I would rather be an educated bum and understand what is going on around me than an ignorant bum," Dr. Weaver told them. He grew up poor in Alabama and swore that he would never be poor again. His mission in life is helping others learn how to make money and have a great life.

Chapter Four
Envy- Bruce

"Socialism is a philosophy of failure, the creed of ignorance, and the gospel of envy, its inherent virtue is the equal sharing of misery," Winston Churchill. (2)

Bruce and Pat went to college together at James Madison University. They are like brothers and enjoyed chasing women, studying hard, and getting great jobs after the college experience.

Bruce is a diesel mechanic at the Ford dealer in Hamburg. He is divorced and twenty-eight years old. He married a sexy woman with a cheating heart while he was in the Navy. She had a great time when he went to sea with the fleet out of Norfolk for three months.

He pulled four years in the Navy and then completed two years learning how to work on diesel engines from the Ford Motor

Company. He is a hard worker and makes good money at the dealership. His weakness is that he always wants what others have.

There are four levels of mechanics at the dealer with different pay grades attached to them. An opening came up the other month and his envy hurt him. His boss overheard him explaining how he deserves more money than his co-worker at the same level.

When a mechanic at a higher level quit suddenly, the boss gave the promotion to the co-worker who works hard and does not complain like Bruce. He is learning to self-regulate and keep his mouth shut sometimes. He must let his work speak for itself at the dealership.

"How do you like it?" Bruce asks.

"Well, it has a certain understated stupidity," Ginger replied.

They are discussing a wall hanging he put up in the barn. It states "Gun Control Means Using Both Hands." They live upstairs in seven different apartments and downstairs there are eight stalls used to store farm equipment, ATVs, lawnmowers, and dirt bikes.

"Was that your ex-wife I saw last week?" Ginger inquired.

"Yes, she wants to get back together and still calls me Poo Bear. That was her pet name for me many years ago. Somehow she found out my new address here," Bruce said.

"Would you ever get back with her? She is sexy," Ginger said.

"There is no way in hell I would get back with her. She is very unstable and frisky. It is all about the money for her. I thank God for getting rid of her," Bruce said.

The Cars song "Just What I Needed" from 1978 is playing on the barn stereo. Tammy loves that music from a long time ago.

"Did she have the nose ring when you were married?" Ginger asks.

"No, no. That is very nasty and looks like some mucus discharge coming out her nostrils. I have to look away from her face to speak to her now," Bruce explains.

"I can believe that. So many people are getting those now. I guess it is easier to remove than a tattoo. So that is good. At least she has that going for her," Ginger said.

"I guess you are correct. I am just thinking that twenty years from now I would regret getting a nose ring or tattoo," Bruce said.

"Amen to that. I will keep my skin free from piercings and ink. The human body is a work of art without that odd crap," Ginger said.

"Did I tell about visiting the rich guy around the corner? He hit a coal vein back in the 1980s and made a million dollars. He and his young wife live in that huge house over close to the high school," Bruce said.

"Yeah, I met the wife at the Boyer's grocery store in Frackville. She looks to be about 40 years old. She said she was a waitress for a long time," Ginger said.

"Really? He is about 60 years old and loves whiskey. I walked in to his den the other day to see if his tractor is working okay after I fixed it. His wife was on the floor clipping his toenails. He was sipping whiskey in a recliner," Bruce said.

"That is gross. It looks like they would stop that while you were there. Put some shoes on! If I ever get married, the husband will be clipping his own toenails," Ginger said.

"It was a wild scene for sure. He offered her up to clip my toenails. It was hilarious. She really wanted to help out. They both seemed tipsy at 3 in the afternoon," Bruce said.

"I wonder if she would give me a pedicure. Ask her the next time she cuts your nails. Can she color my hair?" Ginger asks.

"He told me that he and a friend owned construction equipment and dug around for coal. They came up empty after 1-2 years. The friend sold his half of the equipment and got a real job. A couple months later the rich guy hit it big. I wish I could hit it big like that guy and buy a huge house like that," Bruce said.

"I have learned the secret of being content in any and every situation," Philippians 4:12 Paul realized that contentment is not natural, it is learned. (8)

"Mother, A mother is the holiest thing alive." The engraving in stone is beneath the Whistler's Mother Statue in Ashland, Pennsylvania. The statue depicts James Whistler's mother with a humorless expression in a long dress. It is a monument built in 1937 to honor the mothers of all the coal miners.

It actually honors all mothers and the inscription is from the poet Samuel Taylor Coleridge. Ginger and Bruce are at the statue to see what it is about. They have seen it from the road many times, but never stopped to check it out.

"It is a beautiful statue of bronze and granite. I wonder how long it took them to build it," Ginger said.

"Yeah, it is awesome. She looks so serious and perhaps irritated or sad," Bruce said.

An old couple are sitting on a bench. They are holding hands. She has long gray and black hair. You can tell that she used to be pretty. The old man is unshaven and wearing sweatpants. His mouth hangs open.

"How are you? This warm weather is nice," Ginger says to the couple.

"Yes, we do not like the cold so much anymore. Are you tourists?" the old lady asks.

"No, we live in the barn over in Ashland with the Browns. We were just curious about this huge statue up here on the hill," Bruce explains.

"Yes, they did a good job building this thing. I worked in the coal mines for thirty years. I have trouble with my lungs and had to retire early," the old man said.

"How old do you think this man is?" the old lady asks.

"Well, I hate to guess someone's age. I do not want to insult anyone," Bruce said.

"Oh no, you will not insult anyone. Just take a guess at how old my husband is?" the old lady asks again.

"Okay, he has a great head of hair. How about seventy years old?" Bruce said.

"He is eighty-three years old this month. Doesn't he look great?" the old lady asks.

The old lady just beams looking at her husband. He loves the attention and conversation. You can tell that they do not get out of the house much and really enjoy talking to others.

"Wow, he does look great for eighty-three! What is your secret? I thought you were here on spring break," Bruce said joking around.

"Well, I eat a lot of vegetables and we walk sometimes," the old man said.

"You know both our grandfathers died in the coal mines. It was very dangerous work back in the day. And the pay was never good," the old lady said.

"I bet it was dangerous for sure. I have read stories of workers dying. Did you ever get claustrophobic?" Ginger asks.

"No, no, the tight spaces never bothered me. I used to drive the jeep in the coal mines. I saw many men get injured and saw some die down there. My friend Harry lost two fingers on the cart one day," the old man explains.

The old couple look at each other often during the conversation and you can feel their love from twenty feet away. They thank God for each other. Her face and smile are very pleasant in the afternoon sun. She looks much younger than her age.

"I am seventy-six. But sometimes I feel like I am eighty-three," the old lady jokes.

Many citizens of this part of Pennsylvania worked in the coal mines. It was back breaking work for little pay or benefits for the uneducated men. There are only a few mines operating now.

Ginger and Bruce leave the monument to mothers and decide to stop at the diner in Ashland for a milk shake. The couple makes the best shakes in a small diner that is attached to their house by an odd walkway.

"A co-worker the other day told me a funny story about her old mother sending odd text messages," Ginger said.

"Really? I guess it is hard to have a misunderstanding on social media and in text messages," Bruce said.

"The woman I work with is fifty-six years old. Her mother is eighty years old and lives in South Carolina. She loves the warm weather, Kris Kristofferson, and the beach," Ginger said.

"I love that part of the country. The seafood is to die for. The indigenous folks usually say hello and chat with the tourists," Bruce said.

"The mother is on her fourth husband and he had a stress test the other day. During a stress test you must walk fast or run on a tread mill to check your heart. Her husband has a history of heart trouble," Ginger said.

"He passed. On way home," is the text she sent to her daughter the day of the stress test.

"My co-worker became so worried and wondered if the test was the end of the husband. She called the mother, but she did not answer," Ginger said.

"Wow, I can see how she thought the guy died. I would have visions of the mother crying and trying to process the situation after reading that text," Bruce said.

"Her sister finally found out that the old guy passed the stress test and did not expire as they say and called my co-worker. They had a good laugh after that," Ginger said.

"That is a good one. I think many older people struggle with text messages and emails. That would be a good book idea. You could put a bunch of odd and funny texts and emails in the book," Bruce said.

"The mother has a life-size cardboard cutout of Kris Kristofferson that she sits in the passenger seat of her Smart car. He is buckled in and everything. It is the supreme, creepy fan experience," Ginger said.

"She must love the old, ugly man and his tunes. That is too much. Perhaps some counseling is in order. A stuffed teddy bear may help also," Bruce said.

Vivian and Zeb are sitting out on their upper porch and reading the news. She reads the news online and he reads the paper version of the Wall Street Journal. The electronic bug zapper is working to kill gnats, mosquitoes, and flies every now and then.

"What do you think of all these politicians trying to get elected? I wonder how many are good and how many are bad. It is hard to believe the dumb things they say," Zeb said.

"I think that the women running should act like women and not act like men. You want to be authentic," Vivian said.

"I am with you on that. Voters can tell when you are faking. Your true colors will always come out whether you like it or not," Zeb said.

"Yes, it is the same when you order the burger at the fast food restaurant. You want the real meat and not the fake meat," Vivian said.

She is old school and refuses to try the imitation meat made out of soybeans or other ingredients. She read that the meat is very high in sodium and unhealthy. Vivian only eats real cow, pig, and chicken.

"Well I never thought about politicians and hamburgers together before. But you raise a good point. Actually you raises two good points in an odd way," Zeb said.

"Thank you. You know sometimes I am so smart. It scares me. My brain functions at a high level. I am much smarter than you. It really does scare me sometimes," Vivian said.

"You are so sweet. How did you get so sweet? You are ruining my self-esteem," Zeb said.

Two small deer run through the front yard. The two big barns are across the front yard in the distance. The red and white sides of the barns are very bright in the afternoon sun. There are gun shots coming from the woods behind the barns. The neighbors have a target range over there.

Vivian and Zeb walk over to the neighbor's farm where the brothers are shooting pistols and rifles. One brother just got out of prison and has many prison house tattoos. He is very outgoing and has no boundaries.

"Boy, you targets are so small. I do not think I could hit any of them. I bet you hunters can hit everything," Zeb said.

"No, no, we are just country boys and no experts. Bobby around the corner is an expert. He was a sniper in the Army a long time ago," the brother said.

While Zeb and one brother are chatting the prison brother strikes up a conversation with Vivian. Zeb is chatting and can barely hear the other conversation.

"Where are you from? You are a beautiful woman," the tattooed brother said.

"I am an American citizen. I grew up in China. We moved here from Harrisburg two years ago," Vivian said.

Vivian and Zeb walk back to their farm. The tall trees are very beautiful in greens and browns. Squirrels are everywhere. Rabbits are rushing around.

"Did that guy tell you that you are beautiful? I was talking with his brother, but thought I heard him say that" Zeb said.

"Yes, I did not expect that. He is so funny. I wondered if you heard that. I bet he has never seen an Asian woman around here," Vivian said.

The brothers grew up and remain in Ashland. They never travel and love hunting, shooting, and riding all terrain vehicles. Beer is their constant companion. The work hard at blue collar jobs and hate big government.

"Did you see the girlfriend? She was wild looking. That must be suntan cream. I think she was picking her nose all the time," Zeb said.

"Yes, her skin is dark and tanned. I bet she lays under a suntan booth all the time. That has to be bad for the epidermis. Most women in China would never do that," Vivian said.

"The one brother calls her carrot top. I guess she is his girlfriend. She was chugging down the beers. She is in great shape though," Zeb said.

The brothers are very nice, but suspicious of strangers. They do not trust outsiders in coal country. Their father passed many years ago and owned a bar where the wild folks spent a lot of time. Coal miners used to have a beer or two every night after their shifts down in the mines.

Many of the workers were functioning alcoholics and their wives got really mad at them for blowing most of their wages on beer every week. You do not see many miners around here anymore. Most of the mines shut down because of cheap natural gas and fracking.

"Did you call Verizon about that extra charge on our bill?" Vivian said.

"Yes, it was a frustrating experience with the young guy on the phone. He kept asking me to repeat things. He said he was multi-tasking," Zeb said.

"Yeah, right. They call it multi-tasking. When they say that it really means that they are not doing anything well. I had that when I called the cable company last week," Vivian said.

"I have noticed that many young employees at the fast food joints and on customer service lines cannot perform very simple tasks. They make so many mistakes making coffee or answering questions," Zeb said.

"I noticed that too. This young woman could not even perform simple math at the KFC in Pottsville. I wonder why they make so many mistakes. Is it that they do not care or just lacking knowledge and skill?" Vivian said.

"I do not know, but the employees at Dunkin Donuts cannot even make a cup of coffee with cream. They keep adding sugar for no reason. Sometimes they forget the cream. The task is so simple," Zeb said.

"On the good side, I guess most of our young people are smart and hard working. The kids at Chick-fil-A are great and very professional," Vivian said.

"They keep their restaurants clean. The founder S. Truett Cathy was a great leader and devout Christian. He ran a tight ship. I love that," Zeb said.

"His family still owns and runs the place. Yes, that Bible cannot be beat for giving great advice on living and how to treat others. Thank God for kind and Christian people," Vivian said.

"I bet many people are getting welfare with free apartments and food and do not care about working hard and doing a good job. An old veteran in Frackville told me that his neighbors sit on their porch getting high all day and laugh about people going to work," Zeb said.

"Do you remember those Amish people who built our house in Harrisburg? They worked so hard and did a fabulous job. Remember they told us how they rejected government interference and welfare and things like that. They have a great culture," Vivian said.

"Yes, the old guy was impressive. I think his name was Elam King. He was still so strong at age 80. They were hard workers. He used to take an Amtrak train to Mexico for surgery," Zeb said.

"I heard him say that the medical folks in Mexico charged a lot less than in the United States," Vivian said.

"He said right before his knee surgery the playful brother of the surgeon asked if he could have his dog if anything went wrong during the procedure," Zeb said.

"Yes, the gathered around in a circle and prayed to God and Jesus that the surgery would go well. They prayed for Elam and his family. That was so sweet," Vivian said.

"Elam said the buildings and campus down there are spotless and look brand new. It is just a long way to go for surgery, but the prices are about half the prices here with the greedy doctors, nurses, insurance companies, and hospitals," Zeb said.

"I wonder if the Amish folks worry about all the kidnappings down in Mexico. I read that sometimes the gangs will threaten to cut of a finger or toe for ransom," Vivian said.

"Yes, some guy from California got drunk down there and woke up on an IV. He was missing a kidney! I guess they harvest organs from tourists and sell them around the world," Zeb said.

Bruce is laying on his bed in his apartment in the barn. He thinks back to the road trip he took with Pat during college. They drove from Harrisonburg, VA to Charlotte, NC for an Edwin McCain concert. They love the rock and roll.

They stop for a burger meal in Danville, VA en route to Charlotte. Pat pulls out into traffic on Riverside Drive. It is a four lane divided highway with many stoplights and thick traffic. All of a sudden, a car slams into the passenger side of Pat's small car.

"Wow! What was that? That idiot is out of control! Did you see him? I think that was a Ford Escort," Pat said.

"Oh my God! Are you okay? I think it was a white Lexus, but I am not sure. Call 911!" Bruce said.

A few seconds later another car slams into the rear of Pat's poor little car. It is a state trooper with his lights going and siren blaring. He is chasing a criminal known for dealing drugs.

"What the hell was that? It is a cop. I guess he was chasing a criminal," Pat said.

The young cop walks around the side of Pat's car. He is sweaty and very excited about his chase.

"Are you okay? Damn! I was trying to cut him off. I am sorry. Are you alright?" the cop said.

The cop runs back to his car that is behind Pat's. He makes the radio call to dispatch about the incident.

"Yeah, he hit another car at the intersection of Riverside Drive and Piney Forest Road. He is headed west on Riverside. I will pursue; request backup," the cop says to the dispatcher.

The cop drives off after the criminal. The Danville Rescue Squad medics and another policeman arrive at the scene of the accidents. Pat's car is smashed all along the passenger side and in the rear. It is totaled and cannot be driven. Pat and Bruce are standing in the median and are stiff, but have no visible injuries.

"Are you in any pain? Lay down on the stretcher. Do not move your head. Just take it easy," the medic said.

They are taken to the hospital for x-rays and a good checkout. The medics, Billy and

Laura, are very nice and caring. They ensure that the victims are transported and treated. Pat and Bruce thank God for the kind, caring, and professional medics from the Danville Rescue Squad.

A couple hours later the state trooper walks into the emergency room to talk with Bruce and Pat. They are shaken up and stiff, but do not have any broken bones or lacerations. They lay in beds chatting about the whole situation. They are restless to get back on the road and try to make it to the concert on time.

"I am so sorry for hitting you. I just started sliding in the corner while I was chasing him. My backup arrested him down near Yanceyville on Highway 86. He is a known drug dealer driving his mother's car. He was disarmed and taken to the city jail," the state trooper explains.

"What kind of car was he driving? Was that a Lexus? What an idiot!" Bruce said.

"It was a 1980 Lexus," the cop said.

"I told you it was a Lexus! You owe me dinner. I always wanted a Lexus, but never had one," Bruce says to Pat.

They have to answer some basic questions and then are released from the hospital. The cop takes them to a car rental place and they drive to Charlotte just in time for an awesome concert by Edwin McCain. The opening act is two young guys with dread locks. They are dirty, sweaty, and dressed in t-shirts and shorts.

The band members are Caucasian, but their voices sound like African Americans. They yell and scream and bang on drums. It is just one hour of yelling and drums. They cannot play any other instruments. They are amazingly good and the crowd loves it.

The band makes odd noises. They have pot symbols on their shirts. They wear sandals for the performance. This band is headed nowhere. Fame and riches will elude them.

"What do you think of the band? They are hilarious. I cannot believe this is the opening act," the American man asks his Chinese American wife sitting next to Pat and Bruce.

"They are hard workers! I hope Edwin McCain is better and not like this," the wife says in a serious and thoughtful tone. She struggles to figure out why the crowd likes this odd performance consisting of screaming and hitting drums. This is considered noise where she came from. It is to be avoided at all cost. Why do people pay money to listen to this in America?

Bruce shares their accident story with an older woman at the concert. The woman then goes off on a rant about how the police, prosecutor, and judge should put the criminal in prison and harvest his organs as punishment.

"They should put all violent criminals in prison for a long time. They should force them to donate kidneys and other organs because they hurt other folks. That would be my idea of justice; an eye for an eye," the odd woman explains at the concert.

She is sixty years old with white pigtails. She is overweight and wears a flower print halter top with pink leggings and sandals. Her shirt says 'My Grass Is Blue' on it and her breath smells like Doritos and vodka. She stares at Bruce's butt and thinks nobody notices.

Chapter Five
Gluttony- Mary

"Gluttony is not a secret vice," Orson Welles.

Zeb and Vivian walk from the house to the pond to visit their birds. They have seven Brown Chinese geese, four Peking ducks, and fourteen Muscovy ducks. Each group has its own personality.

The geese are the loudest and most aggressive. They think they own the pond and peck at the others to get out of their way. They are the biggest species at the pond also.

The Peking ducks are pretty loud and have adopted a mallard. They love to dive into the water and look for worms. They are bullies to the Mallards and chase them out of the water all the time.

The Muscovy ducks are so quiet and cute. They gather around any human who visits the pond. They love cracked corn and would hang out with Stalin to get it. They are passive and peaceful and try to stay away from the bossy geese.

The ducks and geese love to insert their necks and torso into the water and paddle with their webbed feet to look for worms and other food. Their butts stick up toward the sky and is so funny for the humans to watch. Some of the birds dive into the water and stay down for ten to twenty seconds at a time.

Mary is sitting on the picnic bench at the pond when Vivian and Zeb get there. She is enjoying coffee and some donuts from Dunkin Donuts. She struggles with her weight and meeting men. She is very sweet and volunteers at the retirement home in Shenandoah.

"Good morning! Four geese were on the road when I came down. I corralled them back into the pasture. I would offer you a donut, but I just ate the last one. I love Dunkin Donuts," Mary said.

"Great, thank you. I wonder where they are getting out. I hope nobody runs them over in their car. People drive too fast around here," Zeb said.

"Yes, the neighbor's dogs were barking at them and they were frightened," Mary said.

After a few minutes of watching the birds splash in the water and get into disputes Vivian and Zeb walk back up the hill through the pasture to the house.

"Did you notice her going through the donuts so fast when we approached the pond?" Vivian asks.

"Yes I did. She looked like a squirrel frantically eating nuts," Zeb said.

"She is great with the kids and animals and just eats too much. I wonder why she is obsessed with food," Vivian said.

"She is an excellent teacher. She won teacher of the year at the North Schuylkill County Elementary School last year. She must be great at helping the kids learn about this world," Zeb said.

"Perhaps I will get her to help me in the garden for some exercise. We can dig and plant and have fun and then go out for lunch," Vivian.

"You may want to skip the last event. I bet she just needs a companion or purpose to get moving and stay in shape," Zeb said.

A few minutes later Mary rings the doorbell to the main house. She is carrying a huge box of donuts.

"I thought you may enjoy some donuts on this beautiful Saturday morning," Mary said.

"She is so sweet. Donuts are expensive and I know she does not make much money at the school. I will take her to Boscov's and buy her a nice outfit soon," Vivian said.

"Thank God for kind and caring people like Mary! We are so lucky to have all the kids in the barn. They are doing great. Let us always help them. They are so strong," Zeb said.

Zeb cranks up "Back in Black" by AC/DC on his phone with earphones on while mowing the lawn. Vivian hates his music. He zips around very fast on the John Deere zero-turn mower. He loves the machine and even bought the John Deere T-shirt.

Vivian gets Mary from the barn and drives to the mall down in Saint Clair. They are walking around looking a nice dress and coat for school.

"Did I tell you met a guy? He teaches math at my school and is very shy. His name is Paul," Mary said.

"Really? That is great. There are so many nice guys out there. What is he like?" Vivian said.

"He is thin and neat and has outstanding manners. He said he likes big women. All the women in his life are large. He has two sisters and one brother. He opens doors and stuff like that for me. He makes me feel special," Mary said.

"He sounds very good with the manners. So many women put up with jerks nowadays. The hookup culture is bad," Vivian said.

"I do not know if I told you that I think I eat just to fight the boredom and loneliness. I have already lost ten pounds since meeting Paul," Mary said.

Mary finds a beautiful professional dress, shoes, and coat at Boscov's. Vivian told her that money is no object and loved helping her out. There is something special about two generations hanging out together and talking. This is the way it used to be before the internet came along in the 1990s.

Vivian is thinking about the article she read about orphans and how many feel an emptiness forever when they do not connect with their parents or past. She loves all of the kids in the barn and treats them like her own son.

Some older folks in Zimbabwe set up "Friendship Benches" in the public places in order to meet and give advice to the youngsters struggling with different issues. The poor nation has been ruined by corrupt and lazy politicians. Sometimes the older people help out with cash too.

Mary is back on the deck in the barn talking with Donald. They are taking it easy after a day of work.

"I saw a great custom truck today in Frackville. It was green and had the guy's name in chrome on the front," Mary said.

"What do you mean? He chromed his name on the front grill? What is his name?" Donald asks.

"Yeah, the guy's name 'MACK' was huge on the front grill. It must of cost a fortune to order that," Mary said.

Donald starts laughing when he realizes that the truck brand name was on the front.

"I hate to be the one who tells you, but MACK is a brand name for big trucks. You are crazy!" Donald explains.

They have a good laugh and see some rabbits running around next to the barn. Some of them look like babies and others are huge. They are eating and so pretty.

"I want to tell you about my part-time job. I work at that reptile zoo in Bloomsburg. We get free food while we are working. It is great," Mary said.

"That sounds awesome. I never had free food on the job," Donald said.

"We have an albino crocodile. He is very cool. The customers cannot believe it. My co-worker has a kimono dragon tattoo on his neck," Mary said.

"That is amazing. Who would get a tattoo like that? I bet the customers do not miss that one," Donald said.

"He is not the sharpest tool in the shed. I bet he felt some serious pain during the tattoo process. Do you know how many nerve endings are up there?" Mary said.

"I would pay to watch someone get a tattoo like that. They could probably sell tickets for it," Donald said.

"A customer came in last weekend with sagging pants. That is not too odd, but this was a white guy about thirty-five years old.

He was bald already. Now that was odd," Mary said.

"Yes, usually only the young guys wear their pants down low like that. I guess they are not smart enough to focus on holding their pants up and learning about this world in college or on the job at the same time," Donald said.

"I bet most business owners or managers would not hire us if our underwear was showing during the interview. You will never see my underwear outside the apartment," Mary said.

"Well let me tell you about the woman I saw in the Saint Clair Walmart. She had on a baby blue short skirt, baby blue top, and fake fur coat. Her skirt and cowboy boots had long tassels flying around. She must have been sixty years old. It was a wild scene," Donald said.

"You do not see tassels anymore. It is a shame. I guess they are popular out west. I love to see different and creative outfits. I am hungry. How about a donut? I love the chocolate cream," Mary said.

"The best part about seeing the lady with the awesome baby blue tassels was in the parking lot. The front bumper of her car had a custom license plate. It reads 'Mama Sassy," Donald said.

Mary drives to the St. John the Baptist Polish National Church in Frackville for the 11:00 am service. The congregation is so nice and welcoming. Many Polish families moved to Frackville back in the 1800s. She sits with her friend Sharon and she has some news.

"You will not believe this one. My friend Jane just gave birth to a baby boy. She and her boyfriend did not even know she was pregnant," Sharon said.

"I heard about the baby. My co-worker knows Jane. How do you not know you are pregnant?" Mary asks.

"Well that is what they are telling everyone. She was always a little chubby and she did not look pregnant when I saw her a few weeks ago. She had some seizures and went into labor," Sharon said.

"Is her boyfriend that derelict who stands beside Highway 61 in Pottsville all day in odd clothing? He is a freak," Mary said.

"Yes, the last time I saw him he was wearing lime colored sweatpants with a towel draped around his neck. He wears a thick gold chain necklace and fake diamond earring. He has a huge Scooby-Doo tattoo on his bicep and loves tanktops. His skinny little arms hang out," Sharon said.

"You know Jane's mother is an orphan and lost her house a few years ago. She and her boyfriend were drunk and high all the time. They lost their jobs and were homeless for a while," Mary said.

"I bet Jane knew she was pregnant and hid it because that fool of a boyfriend would run away from any responsibility. I hope the kid does not look like him. He has the ugly gene," Sharon said.

"He actually thought that brown cows give brown or chocolate milk. Can you believe that? Would you like to go get a chocolate milk shake and a peanut butter pie after church? He has the dumb gene" Mary said.

"Oh yeah! I was dreaming of that last night. Let us go to the diner in Shenandoah," Sharon said.

"After the milk shake, let us go by Boscov's at the mall. They have a big sale on leggings," Mary said.

"Yes, I want to find some with flowers or cartoons. I saw some leopard prints the other day that were fabulous," Sharon said.

"I like the see through or maybe black and white stripes. The camouflage with stomach compression technology would be wonderful. I really need that," Mary said.

"That just sounds right. I have not seen that kind anywhere," Sharon said.

"I wonder if they have free coffee and those big donuts in the church basement? They had a huge spread last week up here," Mary said.

"What did they name that baby? I bet they came up with something good and unusual," Sharon said.

"They actually named the child Billy Bocephus Williams after Hank Williams Junior. Can you believe that? Their last name is Williams," Mary said.

"Well, they pretty much mapped out his future with a name like that. They must love that country music redneck. I never met a doctor, CEO, or successful business man named Billy Bocephus," Sharon said.

The two friends go out to lunch and end up back at the barn. They are watching a documentary about old, ugly rock and roll musicians. They speak on TV about having a great time writing songs, making tons of money, and touring around the world. Of course they ruminate about drugs, alcohol, and having too many sex partners.

"These people are so talented with the music, but so dumb about everything else. It seems like they would watch the money rolling in and prevent theft," Sharon said.

"I know, they got ripped off by so many greedy business people. It is amazing. Did they not know to read the contract before signing it? I think it is funny to hear the old women advise the young women to not use their bodies to get ahead," Mary said.

"That is hilarious. One of them talked about eye candy being a bad thing. It looks like she enjoyed and benefited from being eye candy many moons ago," Sharon said.

"Yes, and some of the old ladies still let it all hang out. I saw one of them on TV in a low cut lace top. It was not a good look with the old and sagging skin," Mary said.

"Let us make a pact that we will cover up really well after age forty. Cleavage should be buried after our youth," Sharon said.

Mary is walking around the farm on the perimeter trails. She is always amazed at how so many trees die or fall during the winter. She notices many dead trees that fell into other trees and lean there for years. Eventually the rot and fall to the ground.

The woodpeckers love the dead trees. Mary listens to them peck and peck during her walks. She thanks God for these wide open spaces without people to dodge or chat with. Zeb cut trails around the farm with a chain saw and ax when he and Vivian bought the place.

Mary sees a red fox running and jumping through the trees. It is tiny and beautiful. She wonders how old he is and what he eats. How do they make it through the winters with snow and ice and minus four degrees?

She loves the lack of man-made things out here. There are no mirrors or furniture or televisions to clutter the forest. This is all made by God. She notices some stumps from trees cut down by Zeb. Perhaps someone cut down these trees before Vivian and Zeb bought this pretty farm.

Mary takes deep breaths and loves the fresh air. You will never smell trucks and cars out here. Her yoga instructor encourages her to completely fill her lungs and enjoy solitude. A darker person may view it as loneliness, but not Mary. She talks to herself and to God in the sun.

The leaves are rustling in the trees. Mary loves that sound. The leaves are crackling under the tiny feet of squirrels. She watches them run and dart up trees. She thinks of lost love and how the old lady told her that there is plenty of time for romance and finding a great husband.

Mary hears hawks screeching. She hears birds chirping. This is much better than sitting at work and listening to the co-workers talk trash. It is so nice to not feel the pressure to listen to others and make good comments. This alone time is awesome.

She wonders if her mother would like this walk in the forest. Did her parents live in a big city? Were they farmers or ranchers? For some reason she doubts it. How old were they when they had her? Were they ever married? Perhaps they just hooked up and the pregnancy was a mistake. She will never know anything about her biological parents.

The fat kid from next door rides by on an ATV. She steps off the trail to make way. Mary waves at him just to be nice. She has never met him, but has seen him around the farm. He oddly stares straight ahead and ignores her. What is wrong with him? She will never wave at him again. "F U" is on the back of his dirty t-shirt.

Vivian and Zeb are walking on the trails behind the barn. They are holding hands and having a great time looking at the trees and wild animals.

"I think I will play golf next week. Do you remember how good I was at that silly game? I birdied that par three seventeenth at Hilton Head," Zeb said.

"I do not remember anything like that. I remember your ball was always in the water, in the sand box, or in the ditch. That is what I remember," Vivian said.

"Thanks a lot. You are ruining my self esteem. It took a lot of practice to play golf at that high level. I used to make one eagle per year when I was young," Zeb said.

"I will tell you what. If you can work on your game and win on the PGA tour, I will dress in a sexy dress and run and kiss you on the 18th green like they do on TV. Would you like that? Is that what they do every week?" Vivian asks.

"Bobby Jones's wife would never talk to him like that. You know he won the Grand Slam and created The Masters with Cliff Roberts," Zeb said.

"Well, you are no Bobby Jones. You are nobody," Vivian said.

Mary is walking on the farm and the trails in the woods. She walks down the hill to the pond to watch the birds. About twenty of the ducks and geese are walking around in the muddy area between the neighbor's pond and Vivian's pond.

All of a sudden, all the birds begin running toward the water. Only the mallard can fly because their wings were clipped when they were young. They are loud and get into the pond as soon as possible. Mary looks up at the blue sky to see the problem.

There are three gigantic hawk circling the pond. They are looking for a good lunch. Mary wishes that she had a rifle and could shoot them down. These predators are unwelcome here. A few weeks ago something attacked one of the Muscovy ducks. She had a bloody tail for a few days, but healed. Vivian sprayed her tail with antibiotics from Tractor Supply.

Mary and Bruce hope that the ducks and geese are too big for the hawks to handle. But the mallards are smaller and vulnerable to attack. Perhaps the hawks are looking for food for their offspring.

Mary notices the old retired guy across the road from the pond. He is obese with his shirt off and wearing jean shorts. His gray beard blows in the wind as he enjoys his coffee on the front porch. He has snake and dragon tattoos all over his stomach, chest, and back. He is white as a sheet.

He has a huge Harley-Davidson tattoo on his arm. Mary wonders how he could have such a commitment to a brand. He has been branded with a brand. She ruminates about how much ink it took to decorate this man.

Mary quickly looks away and tries to get the image out of her mind. She has some thoughts about the situation. "Why doesn't he put on a shirt? He really should cover up all that meat and hair at his age. Is that a surgery scar? He would make a great Santa Claus at the mall. He is disgusting."

Mary watches the ducks and geese swim and walk around. They make different noises and roam around looking for insects and worms. They walk over to the duck house for some cracked corn that Zeb and Vivian put out every day. They take small sips of water from the pond to wash down the corn.

She walks back up the hill to the barn. The green trees are so beautiful. The yellow wild flowers are stunning at the tree line. Many tiny birds are flying around. The neighbor's two dogs are barking at the ducks and smelling everything they can. The dog owners only let them outside four times per day. Even dogs get cabin fever.

Chapter Six
Wrath- Donald

"Throw away thy rod, throw away thy wrath; O God, take the gentle path," George Herbert.

Wrath is defined as a strong vengeful anger or indignation or retributory punishment for an offense or crime. (6) It can quickly escalate when one party to a dispute gets mad at the other.

Pope Urban II launched a holy war against Muslims that has since become known as The First Crusade during 1095. (5) Many people died from using military tools in anger instead of using diplomacy, economics, or information to shape the world.

Donald is riding his Harley Davidson down Highway 61 to the Orwigsburg Harley Davidson shop. He rides a 2018 Harley Davidson Breakout that is painted like an American flag. He loves the chrome, growling sound, and fat rear tire. Harley represents American success and quality to him.

He kept a tight lid on spending and splurged for the turbine chrome wheels last year. They shine like diamonds with the bike parked or rolling down the highway. He keeps his ride very clean and even talks to it. There will be no Japanese motorcycles in his garage. American steel is the only way to go for this man.

He loves the 1969 movie "Easy Rider" where one of the hogs is painted like the flag. Donald does not like the drug scenes in the movie and will always run away from anyone with drugs. But he loves Harley-Davidsons and the freedom of the open road in the great United States of America.

Zeb is on his fourth Harley over many decades and loves them too. He loves the wind in his face and zooming down Highway 81 at seventy miles per hour. The freedom is amazing to him. He has so many great memories with family and friends rolling down the road of life.

Vivian bought an electric jacket and gloves for Zeb to ride during the winters. He stays warm in the gear down to 30 degrees in the beautiful mountains of Pennsylvania. Sometimes he gets hot and has to turn down the thermostat.

Donald is going to check on new tires for the hog. Zeb gave him a coupon for a free set of tires for Christmas. All of a sudden, a young man in a damaged Toyota starts tailgating him. Donald sees this dangerous driver in his rear view mirror and shakes his fist at him.

He yells at him, but the dumb driver cannot hear anything through the helmet and the bike's roar. Donald thinks about waving his pistol at the guy, but decides against it and speeds away to safety.

"Why do the police not punish the tailgaters and other reckless drivers? Why don't these people just pass the slower vehicle? They hurt and kill so many innocent people," Donald thinks to himself. He is shaking when he arrives at the hog shop and gets off the motorcycle. The fool could have rammed into him and killed him so quickly.

Donald tells the story to an old biker sitting on the "Liars Bench" outside the dealership and asks what he would have done.

"I just turn the other cheek and get away from dangerous folks like that. I put them out of my mind and just enjoy the ride. Stupid people can really hurt you. Just stay away from them," the old biker says as he combs his long gray beard and enjoys a cigarette without a filter.

The old biker is taking it easy and scratching his stuff. His wife appears from the store with a new T-shirt and they zoom off. He continues with the free advice for the youngster.

"You see son, we have four types of people who can really hurt us. We must take care to avoid being damaged. The types are dumb, evil, greedy, and lazy folks. As Bachman-Turner Overdrive (BTO) said, we must look after number one. And number one is you," the odd biker explains.

"Lookin' Out For #1" by BTO comes on the speakers at the Harley shop. The Canadians sing about looking out for yourself in this brutal world.

Donald is African-American and graduated from James Madison University in Virginia with a bachelors degree in business. He studied hard and enjoyed the ladies very much. The student body is mostly female.

He is a manager at the huge warehouse behind the McDonald's in Frackville now. At his previous job he worked with and began to emulate several older men's behavior. He is great with math and has a ton of common sense.

These older men are judgmental and confront people they disagree with. Donald started having a bad temper and letting tiny things bother him. He has an intense personality and works extremely hard.

Donald thinks back to a time many years ago. He was in a bathroom stall at Cabela's in Hamburg. Two white guys came and started saying terrible things about all black people. They said they are all stupid and lazy.

He wondered how anyone could be so ignorant of a huge group of humans. There are good and bad people in every group. Donald will always work very hard because that is what the Bible suggests and because that is how he is so successful in his short life.

Sometimes he cries at night in his room in the barn thinking about the void that is his missing parents. Did they abandon him? Did they get murdered? He wants to prove to everyone how strong, moral, and successful he is.

"Did I tell you about my date last week? I took a girl out I met online," Donald said.

"No, was she nice? How was the date? It is hard to find people with good hearts around here," Mary said.

"I do not think I will take her out again. She kept talking about how her former boyfriend bought her a car. He gave her a car after only a month of dating. How crazy is that?" Donald said.

"Well, I guess many people view dating as a quid pro quo. They see only benefits and costs. It is sad for sure. You could offer her a skateboard to see how much she loves you," Mary said.

"You are very funny. She also had a tongue ring. She chipped her tooth with that dumb thing. The search continues," Donald said.

"Did you see that dating app? A college girl came out with a funny app for dating. She sent it to her ex-boyfriends. It is kind of a survey just for laughs. The questions are like the following," Mary said.

1. What did you enjoy about dating Mary?
2. How could Mary make the date more enjoyable?
3. What is wrong with Mary?
4. What is wrong with you?

"That is hilarious. It is interesting to go out on dates. People are so different and make wild assumptions about behavior and other people," Donald said.

Sometimes Donald lashes out at others and then retracts the aggressive statement and apologizes. He is trying to control his anger, but it is difficult to change.

Some people say that a hot temper reveals a cold heart. That is not always true. It is so easy to speak without thinking when a rude person comes along. Donald is working on it in his own time. He has a huge heart and helps people all the time with money and deeds.

Anger is often below the surface and ready to strike. Resentment silently corrodes the core of our thoughts. It's when the thoughts that fill up our minds are true, noble, right, pure, lovely, admirable, and praiseworthy that we keep Jesus's peace in our hearts. (7)

Donald is enjoying the night sky in a rocking chair on the barn deck late one night. He sometimes daydreams about his parents. He wonders what they looked like and why they abandoned him. Did he have siblings? Do they search for him? Do they give a damn about him?

He looks up at the moon and ruminates about a dream he has had his entire life. The clouds are moving fast tonight covering and then uncovering the moon. A cold front is moving through and the stars are bright. The wind blows the tall trees back and forth.

His recurring dream involves the face of the moon. He imagines the faces of his father and mother on the moon. The white, black, and gray colors form his parents' faces briefly and then vanish. Sometimes he sees their profiles. Other times the moon reveals a frontal view of his parents.

He cries for a while and then manages to smile. He feels such emptiness in his heart from not knowing and spending time with his parents. This haunts him day and night, but he forces himself to think about his wonderful and successful young life.

He thanks God and Jesus for everything good. He thanks them for the lack of anything really bad. Life is great in most respects. Vivian and Zeb are like parents or at least a loving aunt and uncle. Why did this happen to him? Why is he the orphan? Where are his parents?

Donald is at the Boyer's grocery store in Frackville buying some food. It is a small chain with a few stores in this area. He is in line to check out and takes four steps to check out the homemade pastries. An older white guy behind him jumps ahead in the line.

"Hey! What the hell are you doing? I was just getting a couple pies," Donald said.

"Oh, I thought you were leaving the line, sorry," the old guy says as he suddenly realizes that he could be beaten severely by the muscular young man in front of him.

The rude guy backs down quickly and averts his eyes. Other people in the line give him the stink eye and wonder if he is racist. He is a little embarrassed that he tried to cheat by jumping in line. He pretends to read something on his phone and hope this blows over.

Donald pays for his stuff and walks to his vehicle. He thinks about the rude guy and wonders if he is narcissistic. Most serial killers are that way. Is that idiot racist?

Donald wonders if his own reaction was too harsh. He needed to teach this jerk a lesson. He will never take any crap from rude, evil, or ignorant people.

"Perhaps I should have been a little less aggressive, Maybe I can be a gentler person in the future. God help me to be a nicer person," Donald thinks to himself.

He struggles with outbursts when he gets angry at others. He then briefly reconsiders his aggression and then quickly moves on to avoid any embarrassment. He drives home and reads the Bible for guidance. He loves the New Testament and how gentle Jesus was to opponents.

"Change is hard when you get into your twenties. I need to be nicer and always think before I speak or act," Donald says to himself.

He is not too hard on himself because he remembers Keith in college. This lunatic held a used car dealer up against the wall when he tried to rip him off down in Harrisonburg. Donald reassures himself that at least he is mostly non-violent when it comes to unethical people. The dealer tried to sneak in some extra charges on Keith for a used truck.

Donald jumped into the role of hostage negotiator to get Keith to release the poor, unethical car dealer. He was about to get pummeled for cheating his customer. Keith taught him the meaning of respect that day.

His deal is that he wants fairness and equal rights. That is what is in our constitution and that is what he demands. Racism is stupid and unacceptable for anyone in America. Federal, state, and local laws back Donald up on this. Thank God almost all Americans believe in equal rights.

The rest of the day he gives compliment after compliment to everyone he meets. He is so sweet and understanding for a day. Change is hard. He opens doors for people like a bellhop. He acts like there is no tomorrow. He must be a nicer person right now.

Donald thinks about the former mayor of Centralia. He met this nut last week and he is full of rage. He refused to take a lot of government money to sell his old house and move away from the coal mine fires burning beneath his house.

"The government can kiss my ass. I am never moving from my parent's house and home. I will die there and there in nothing the government fools can do!" former mayor of Centralia said.

Donald met the guy at Weis Markets while he was buying groceries. He is still very upset. Some careless people burning trash started a coal mine fire in 1962 and it is still burning hot today. Several companies tried to put it out to no avail.

The fires melted the four-lane highway that ran through there. Street artists and others spray paint all over the highway. Tourists come and see the twisted and ruined highway. There are broken sidewalks and baby dolls from the 1960s in the deserted village.

Many houses were torn down and only two remain. The government plan is to wait out the mayor and another family until they die and then dig up the coal and put out the fires. Several dumb judges and lawyers would not force the holdouts to move over the decades in wasteful lawsuits and counter suits. The Post Office revoked the zip code in 2002.

Donald always takes his visiting friends to Centralia to walk on the forgotten highway.

He shows them where the road is buckled and sunken from the coal mine fires and heat underground. They laugh at the silly and profane graffiti spray painted all over the closed down highway.

Sometimes people are flying drones to video the ghost town and the closed highway. One time there was a street preacher telling everyone that they were going to hell. He was standing on a milk crate and yelling at passersby with a karaoke machine.

Donald likes to see the freaks walking on the highway too. There was the young, chubby woman with her butt hanging out beneath her skirt. There was the bald man with flames tattooed all over his skull. They draw odd things with chalk on the highway.

One time they saw a tent set up beside the guardrail. A couple was obviously frisky and doing things that should only be done in a dimly lit bedroom. Their silhouettes from the sun displayed clearly their activity. They were so loud that the tourist mothers had to corral their children and walk quickly away.

The young tourists were laughing and pointing at the tent. Some were taking video and pictures of this couple lacking in self awareness and self control. Some were smoking pot and were there as long as the couple performed the sideshow.

Donald is back at the barn talking with Dennis who is just back from repairing a power line in Ringtown. He works for the local power company and makes $56 per hour on a bucket truck.

Dennis has worked for the power company for thirty years and has a wife and two boys. He works hard and paid for them to go to Liberty University down in Virginia. Dennis and Kim love guns and God. His middle name is Ford. His father really loved the Ford Motor Company.

"I was talking to the woman who teaches at the community college over there in Ringtown. I asked her if they have a lot of students. I thought the place would be packed," Dennis said.

"I bet they have a lot of low income students. I guess the state owned school is free or almost free and paid for by the taxpayers," Donald said.

"Yes, I thought so too. She said they have to go out and beg the young people to go to college. It is free for most of them. The problem is the parents. They do not believe in education and do not trust strangers," Dennis said.

"They should make the dumb parents work and pay taxes. I bet many of the them do nothing and expect their kids to have the same ridiculous lifestyle. That makes me mad," Donald said.

"I agree with that. It seems like the parents would want their kids to read and learn and escape that severe poverty. I guess they cannot see behind their own unnecessary situation," Dennis said.

"That is a brutal cycle and hard to break. I met many poor and skinny kids at the orphanage. Thank God they made to our great school down in Hershey. They used to tell us how they did not have enough to eat before their parents abandoning them. It was so sad. We should kill the violent and horrible parents," Donald said.

They hear rifles and pistols firing next door. The brothers are practicing at their firing range on the farm next door. They grow corn and soybean and love to shoot weapons.

"I had a great time at the gun rally in Richmond, VA last year. There were guys walking around with automatic weapons. Our founders knew it was important for the citizens to have weapons. We must protect the second amendment for all our might," Dennis said.

"I am with you on that one. I have a concealed carry permit. The government is too big and abusive and will only get worse if the leftists take our weapons," Donald said.

"Well I have to go see my boys. They are home for college break. One graduates this year and the other next year. I thank God for a wonderful family. Kim and I are taking them to Stuckeys for lunch," Dennis said.

"You reminded me of the overweight truck driver we saw at Waffle House last week in Mount Joy. He descended from his tall rig with his butt hanging out over his jeans. His backside was right outside the window at our booth. It was a wild scene. We were trying to eat," Donald said.

Dennis is sucking down his sixth cup of coffee of the day and it is only the afternoon. He loves Tim Horton's brand and tries to drink reduced caffeine coffee when he can. He drives away quickly in his huge Ford pickup.

He thinks about his good father who passed away a long time ago and named him Ford.

Dennis suddenly drives into the big pasture next to the barn. He guns the engine in his truck and starts doing doughnuts in the grass and dirt just for kicks. He thinks about doing doughnuts on his Harley-Davidson many years ago at keg parties in Turbeville, Virginia. He grew up down there. Those were good times. He cranks up "Slow Ride" by Foghat in the truck. Dirt and rocks are flying everywhere.

Donald is laughing and watching Dennis tear up the pasture. He remembers the city kids from New York City he met in Centralia a while back. They never shoot guns, drive ATVs, or spin around in trucks over there.

"You do not get this in the city. What a shame that is. How many doughnuts is he going to do? I bet nobody is doing doughnuts on Long Island right now," Donald thinks to himself.

The pigs are looking at Dennis spin around. His truck is very loud with dual exhaust. They do not know if this represents a threat to them or not. They are very curious about this commotion in the pasture. The baby pigs are hiding behind the parents.

Donald thinks about their conversation and realizes his language was too strong. He should tone down the anger directed toward the lazy people who do not support their children with food or education. He will never agree with them, but must be a nicer and gentler person. He prays to God and Jesus for the strength and wisdom to change.

"Dear God and Jesus help me to be a better person. Help me to find less aggressive words to express my thoughts and feelings. Thank you God for everything and please help the poor and uneducated folks to rise up. Please help all the kids to be Christian and strong," Donald prays to himself.

The neighbor's dogs come out of their house and start barking at the ducks and geese down at the pond. They run around and rush several birds that escaped Zeb's fence and chicken wire. Thank goodness the dogs are all bark and no bite. They could easily catch and kill the birds, but enjoy barking at them instead. The birds cannot fly and are not very fast runners.

Every couple days Vivian and Zeb have to corral the birds and walk them back into the pasture. The birds enjoy walking around the chicken wire and swimming in the neighbor's pond. Zeb ran chicken wire around three sides of the pond, but not across the pasture side.

Sometimes the bad birds have to spend the night in the middle of the neighbor's pond because they are terrified of the dogs. The neighbor lets the dogs out three or four times per day. Vivian and Zeb wonder why the birds are not satisfied to stay in the pasture and their own pond.

The Muscovy ducks love digging around in the mud inside and outside the pasture. The geese and Peking ducks like doing this, but the Muscovy ducks love it the most. Vivian and Zeb are worried that reckless car drivers will kill the birds if they get near the country road next to the pond.

A big deer comes to eat the cracked corn in the duck house early in the mornings. Sometimes she is on the hunting camera down at the pond. It takes and transmits pictures to Zeb's cell phone if it picks up any activity at any time of day. The deer has huge ears and only comes by once every few weeks.

Chapter Seven
Sloth- Patty

"You must avoid sloth, that wicked siren," Horace. (2)

A disinclination to action or labor or a spiritual apathy is the definition of sloth. (6) Have you ever known anyone like that?

The French army officers and soldiers had a moment of weakness or laziness during 1954 because they failed to secure their perimeter on some mountains in Vietnam or Indochina. They secured the main road leading to their camp but should have worked a little bit harder before going to sleep. The Vietnamese came over the mountain and slaughtered them the next day.

January 2020
  Ashland, PA

Mary and Patty are talking on the upper deck of the barn. They love silly conversations that can go on for hours.

"If you were queen, what laws would you dictate to your subjects?" Mary asks.

"I would pass a law to outlaw leggings. I have been traumatized so many times by this clothing," Patty explains.

"That is a good one. I have seen old men and women wear those things. It is unfortunate and very nasty. Some people call them yoga pants, but most people wearing them I am quite sure do not even know what yoga is," Mary said.

"I saw a young, gigantic woman in Walmart in pink and black leggings with a pink hat on. She looked like a very well dressed and colorful tick," Patty said.

"I remember that the founder of Lulemon blamed fat women when their shoddy tights ripped open at the crotch. I think they ran him off, but he brings up a good point," Mary said.

"The see-through leggings have to go. I see too much meat hanging out," Patty said.

"I want to ban selfies. Everywhere I turn they are there. I see too many turkey necks, wrinkles, and food between less-than-perfect teeth. Perhaps we could ban selfies closer than ten feet," Mary said.

"I would support that. Maybe we should ban closeup selfies for those over fifty years old. Or we can ban selfie sticks shorter than ten feet," Patty said.

Zeb and Vivian are sitting on their front porch and enjoying the view. They love the wide open spaces and the birds flying all around. Zeb picked up two rocking chairs from the Cracker Barrel and loves them. Vivian thinks he paid too much. The temperature rose into the 60s the last couple days. Several hawks and geese just flew by the barn.

"I saw some of the Muscovy ducks walking around on the ice on the pond last week. I wonder why they like to slide and walk on the ice. They are so cute and quiet," Vivian said.

"They are very cute. Boy, I noticed when the temperature drops they eat more and more cracked corn," Zeb said.

The high temperatures can range from minus four degrees to positive 65 degrees from November until March in Ashland. The range is more like highs in the 90s and lows in the 50s during the Spring, Summer, and Fall.

"Do you think humans should have four legs instead of two. We should have two going down and two pointed up. That way we could switch between up and down every couple days and prevent sagging," Vivian said.

"Is that the best idea you have? Have you been watching the science fiction shows too much?" Zeb said.

"I was thinking about the aging process and everything sagging. It is very sad. Your butt is already almost dragging on the ground," Vivian said.

"You are so sweet. I can get some work done. I can get a butt lift soon and some Botox if that helps," Zeb said.

"I think it is too late for you. How about an assistant husband? You suggested that a couple months ago," Vivian said.

"No, no, I can handle the workload and be your sexy farmer," Zeb said.

Patty walks over from the barn to the porch to visit with Vivian and Zeb. She is short and chubby and works at Walmart in the deli.

"How are you two? Thank you so much for the $600 last week. I paid off my car insurance with it. I saw you enjoying this warm day over here. This place is paradise with all the animals and mountains. I had a bad day at work and I want your thoughts," Patty said.

"This warm weather is great. What happened at the Walmart? People seem to love that place," Zeb said.

"My co-worker and I were talking trash in the break room they other day. We were saying how easy it is to hide and take it easy at work," Patty said.

"I wondered about that. It seems like many workers at Lowe's hide to avoid helping me load stuff on the truck," Zeb said.

"We did not realize that the day shift manager of the entire store was in the break room. I think he heard us because he promoted another person in the deli to the manager position. Suzy and I were sure one of us would get the promotion," Patty said.

"Well you will probably get the next promotion. Just keep your head down and work harder. You have been there a long time," Zeb said.

"The Bible says that Jesus worked very hard as a carpenter and telling everyone about God and the good news. I think all of us should try to emulate Jesus," Vivian said.

"Why do their bathrooms smell so bad? It really stinks in there. The clorox is right there in the grocery section," Vivian said.

"Yes, the men's restroom smells like a septic tank or sewer. I noticed the criminals cut off tags and steal stuff in there," Zeb said.

"Maybe I will mention that at our store meeting. I need to change the manager's perception of me too," Patty said.

"I love the organic apples from Fiji. I am surprised they have enough land to grow apples on Fiji. I think the little island is sinking," Zeb said.

This area of Pennsylvania is 95% Caucasian. Zeb and Vivian joke about the lack of diversity sometimes.

"I saw another Asian woman in Walmart the other day. I almost had a stroke, but did not have the chance to talk to her," Vivian said.

Someone in the barn blares "Stairway to Heaven" on the stereo. The Led Zeppelin classic entertains everyone but Vivian.

"Turn that monkey music down!" Vivian complains.

"I saw a small fox the other day on the trails. He was red and dancing through the woods. It was beautiful," Patty said.

"Really? I wonder if it is the same one we saw a couple weeks ago. Was it over near the corn field?" Zeb said.

"Yes, between the corn field and the main trail," Patty said.

"He is beautiful, but I hope he does not kill any of the birds at the pond," Vivian said.

"Peter, the guy next door, showed me a picture of a diseased coyote on his cell phone. He and his neighbors are trying to track it down and kill it. He says it has rabies and is crazy. It looks like a monster," Zeb said.

"I bet our geese would yell at him. They are so bossy and territorial with their pond. They are so loud," Patty said.

"Did they get rid of the blue and yellow vests? Maybe I missed them the last time," Vivian said.

"Yes, the blue and yellow vest is history. I felt like a damn fool in that thing. Some of us got together and burned them after work," Patty said.

"I kind of liked that look. I think I saw that low budget outfit at Sturgis. The bikers love stuff like that," Zeb said.

"If the body be feeble, the mind will not be strong," Thomas Jefferson. (2) Old TJ recommended two hours of physical activity per day.

Have you noticed that some gas stations have black toilets now. What is that about?" Vivian said.

"I bet it saves money on cleaning. You cannot tell if the bowl is clean or dirty now. They can clean it once a week instead of hourly now," Zeb said.

"Well I do not like it. You cannot see if anything bad is in there," Vivian said.

"Perhaps it is an improvement not to see anything down there," Patty said.

"While we are discussing plumbing, I am glad that the hotel owners finally realized after several decades that nobody wants to take a tub bath in a hotel room. They finally removed the tubs and went with showers only," Zeb said.

"That is an improvement. The only person who took the tub bath was that prostitute in that dumb movie Pretty Woman," Vivian said.

"I wonder if some women became hookers because that stupid Hollywood movie made the job look so glamorous," Patty said.

"I see your roommates getting the grill ready over there. You better get yourself back home," Zeb said.

"You know who is a hard worker? That stripper in Texas fell off the fifteen-foot stripping pole and then continued to entertain. Nobody can call her lazy," Vivian said.

"Wow, she is one motivated stripper. I wonder if the other strippers tell her to ease up because she is making them look lazy and cutting their tips," Zeb said.

"You sound like you are talking about those hard working Chinese people in Russia. The Russians complain that they are making them look lazy and taking their jobs," Vivian said.

The barn dwellers get together and have a cookout every week or two. They love to talk about their current lives and to look back on the orphan school days. It is kind of like a Thanksgiving meal every week for these lucky youngsters. They are closer than many biological families.

They throw darts, play bumper pool, shoot pistols, and listen to rock and roll in the barn. Vivian and Zeb provide most of the food and entertainment on the farm for these tenants. Their friends and co-workers cannot believe all the benefits that come from renting an apartment in the barn. Very few landlords give a crap about their renters.

They all completed college and love to swap stories about those days. It is good to be young and successful and free. They talk about the good times and they talk about the bad times.

Patty waters her plants and thinks about a past boyfriend. He loved to walk in gardens and arboretums. He loved to go hiking and biking. She liked those activities, but never loved them. She more into reading and sitting and talking.

One day, the guy out of the blue told her she was just too lazy. He left abruptly at Taco Bell and she never saw him again. Patty thought at the time that he was being too intolerant. She thought he was a jerk.

Now she thinks perhaps she should have bent to his way of thinking. Maybe she should have gotten into more walking and vigorous exercise. Was she wrong? Was she too set in her ways? Was this guy good for her? He did have a nice smile.

Patty wonders if her parents were active folks or sedentary. Maybe one was active the other not active. Did they argue about such things? Were they educated or uneducated? What kinds of jobs did they have? What did they do for fun? Why on earth did they not want her?

Her new years resolution is to be more active. Her cholesterol is too high and the doctor suggested more physical fitness. Patty read an article a while back that reported a higher risk of dementia for sedentary people. She wants no part of that disease.

She wonders if the walker guy has other problems with her. He did not give her a chance to ask. He was out of the restaurant before he even finished the cheap tacos. He and Patty used to enjoy sitting on the deck and chatting about college. Perhaps he was just faking. The more she thinks about the situation the more she believes that he is a jerk. He does not deserve an intelligent and attractive woman like her. He probably has a thin hiker girlfriend now who cheats on him.

She wonders if other animals break up because one is more active than the other. Do squirrels or monkeys split due to such differences? She is sure that the elephant and rhinoceros do not struggle with such matters. But how about snails and snakes.

Sal and Mary are down at the pond sitting at the picnic table. Several people from Gordon come by to see the ducks and geese every week. Vivian's pond is like a local park for them. Zeb and Vivian encourage them to come and feed and look after the birds.

One of the Peking ducks is obsessed with a male mallard. He is chasing the poor mallard around in the water and on land. He wants to keep the mallard out of the pond for some unknown reason.

The mallard can fly, but chooses to run fast most of the time to escape being bitten by the duck. The duck is too fat to fly. Sal and Mary wonder why the duck is so mad at the mallard. Sometimes he chases both male mallards around.

There are two beautiful male mallards with green necks and one female. The female yells and squawks to cheer on her fellow mallards against the evil Peking duck. The Muscovy ducks are docile and swim or walk quickly to avoid the acrimony at the pond.

Mary and Sal are Hispanic folks from Hazleton up Highway 81. He works building houses for the Amish group in the area. They build high quality houses and sheds at lower prices than the regular contractors.

The Hispanic group and Amish group both strongly believe in God and Jesus and work hard. They do not like government and high taxes or regulation. Vivian and Zeb hire them sometimes for projects around the farm.

Sal walks around to the open side of the duck house. A goose is in the corner laying eggs. She looks so vulnerable and sweet. Normally she is loud and chasing the ducks away from the cracked corn. Mary spreads more straw on the ground for the brown Chinese geese.

Many people take the eggs and eat them. Vivian tells everyone to take whatever they want. The goose eggs are huge and delicious. Some neighbors prefer the smaller duck eggs. Vivian loves them all because they are organic. There are twenty-seven birds at the pond and Zeb thinks that is enough.

It is late afternoon and Patty walks to the trail on the perimeter of the farm. She is listening to "I Feel Good" by James Brown on her phone. She watches as the rooster rounds up his hens for the evening. The rooster struts around and has his own harem. He ensures they all of them walk into the enclosure for safety. The farmer next door built a very nice chicken coop and locks the door at night.

The rooster is crowing all the time and looks so proud of himself. Patty is laughing to herself while watching these wild animals in their family unit. She thinks it is so cute that the rooster is taking care of his hens. He knows all about the predators that come out at night and plans ahead for everyone's safety.

Patty ruminates about how we are so lucky to live in this day and age. It is one of the safest times to live. No longer do violent people roam around and kill without consequences. The state and church no long imprison and kill folks for the seven deadly sins. It is rare to die a violent death anymore. She thanks God for the peaceful times. Peace is abnormal in many countries, but it is very normal here in America. Patty notices the trees lining the top of the mountain. It looks kind of like a man's unshaven face with stubble.

"This farm is beautiful. The Earth is so beautiful. Look at those mountains. Thank God women and men are equal here in this little country. Please help us God and have mercy on us," Patty prays to herself.

The seven friends are looking for chairs and Pat walks into the barn office to get a couple rocking chairs for the party. He accidentally hits a cardboard box with a chair and its contents spill onto the concrete floor.

Several old letters with yellowing paper and old stamps are spread out on the floor. He kneels down to put them back into the box and his curiosity gets the best of him. One is from Vivian in China to Zeb in America and is dated March 6th, 2000. It reads as follows.

"I cannot believe that Joe received some of the children of the people on that bus. That is quite a coincidence for sure. God help them. I miss you very much! My family is well and we drove to Shenzen yesterday. I love you and see you in three more weeks!"

Pat reads several of the letters and realizes something he never could have imagined.

Zeb's brother was an alcoholic who somehow kept a full-time job driving a charter bus. He crashed a bus in the mountains of Tennessee in dense fog one morning during 1995. All on board perished.

John, the brother, was drunk at the wheel. Pat discovers the newspaper picture of the crash site inside the box with all the letters in the barn. He wonders why Zeb and Vivian lied about his brother dying young until he reads more of the letters.

Pat figures out that his parents and all of the parents of the seven orphans in the barn were on that bus. They all died because Zeb's brother was drunk at the wheel. That is why it is a secret. Zeb still feels guilty for not intervening to stop his brother from abusing alcohol.

Pat takes the letters upstairs to the others in the barn and explains what he found to the others. They all start reading the letters and information to piece together what happened. They realize that Zeb and Vivian made a pledge to always take care of the orphans of the bus crash.

The orphans see proof that the administrators at the Hershey Orphan School decided to bury the details of their parents. That was the policy at that time for the orphanage.

The seven friends figure out that it is no accident that they are all living in this beautiful barn on this beautiful farm in Ashland, Pennsylvania. All of them used the same referral service at the orphanage to find jobs and apartments in the area.

They sit in the barn dumbfounded by what they have found. They ask many questions and wonder how much of their success is due to Vivian and Zeb. Did they give all that money to support the seven due to guilt from Zeb's brother killing their parents? The orphans feel a little guilty for violating the privacy of Vivian and Zeb by reading their private letters.

Vivian and Zeb have been sending money to the orphanage to help these kids have greats lives despite losing their parents in the bus crash. Zeb must feel guilty that his brother caused all this pain.

Some of the friends are crying and some are just eager for more information. They cannot wait to discuss this with Vivian and Zeb. They just assumed that they were kind and Christian landlords and never dreamed that they are all connected by a horrible bus accident so long ago.

The friends grill and eat steak and potatoes at the barn. Vivian and Zeb stock a huge freezer and refrigerator full of free food for them all year long. They have salads and drink beer late into the night. They wonder if they would ever have known the truth if Pat had not found these letters in the barn office. Were Vivian and Zeb ever going to tell them the truth?

The stars are very bright tonight. The moon is full. The warm glow of lights in the barn are soothing. The friends stare at the tree-covered mountains surrounding the farm. They hang out on the second floor deck of the barn and walk around the outside too. Every and now and then deer run through the fields. The rooster crows on the next farm over. Cute little brown chipmunks with black and white stripes run around between the trees.

They pray to God and Jesus for answers. They thank God for enjoying wonderful lives so far. They thank God for each other and Vivian and Zeb. Should they keep this information to themselves? Should they confront Vivian and Zeb with these revelations? Will they be mad that they read their private letters?

Should they try to find their relatives? Why did this happen to them? The feeling of emptiness from being orphans and not knowing their parents is stronger than ever in their hearts. What does all this mean? What should they do?

Bibliography

1. Wikipedia.org.

2. Brainyquote.com.

3. The Wall Street Journal.

4. Learnreligions.com.

5. Keith Burnside, "Top Ten Worst Popes in History" Toptenz.net 2009.

6. Merriam-webster.com.

7. Cindy Hess Kasper, "Thoughts of Joy" Our Daily Bread 2020.

8. Monica Brands, "The Secret" Our Daily Bread 2020.

9. Joe Posnanski, "The Life and Afterlife of Harry Houdini" Avid Reader 2020.

About the Author

David Xu retired after thirty years in the United States Army, three of which were at the Pentagon. His recent work includes three Easy Eddie humor books and Redneck Dystopia, a political fiction book. He lives on a farm in Ashland, Pennsylvania with his charming wife Nancy who grew up in China. Their son lives on Long Island, New York.

www.ingramcontent.com/pod-product-compliance
Lightning Source LLC
Chambersburg PA
CBHW020615120726
47905CB00003B/807